THE REAPER CHRONICLES

F.T. SCOTT

authorHOUSE®

AuthorHouse™
1663 Liberty Drive
Bloomington, IN 47403
www.authorhouse.com
Phone: 833-262-8899

Published by AuthorHouse 07/01/2021

ISBN: 978-1-6655-3083-5 (sc)
ISBN: 978-1-6655-3088-0 (e)

IN DEDICATION...

To my Grandfather: Without you, this book would not have been possible. Thank you for your wisdom and guidance all these years.

To Crys R.: Thank you for inspiring me to open my mind and be a better person and showing me the way to creativity and beauty. May you be as much of an inspiration to others as you were to me. May our paths cross again one day.

PROLOGUE

THE PRISON SHIP

Elliot slept on the bare metal floor of his cell on a freighter that had been converted into a makeshift prison ship. He awoke to the sound of metal doors opening and closing. Feigning sleep, he listened to the sound of footsteps coming in his direction. His cell door creaked as it opened. Battered and bruised, Elliot was dragged from his cell by one of his legs. He grunted and grabbed at the bars of his cell, trying to fight off his captors. One guard struck him in the head with a blunt object—or maybe a fist or foot, he couldn't tell. His head bounced off the metal floor, and his captors continued to drag him.

"*Elliot*!" yelled Loki, a tribal warrior also being held captive on the prison ship. The paint markings on her face were now faded smudges. She watched helplessly from her cell as Elliot was beaten and dragged.

Elliot shot Loki a determined look and nodded his head.

Loki nodded back and watched Elliot being dragged out of her sight.

Elliot grunted as he was being pulled down a long hall, fighting his captors every inch of the way. One of his captors had had enough, so he turned and struck Elliot in the head with the butt of a rifle, presumably the object he had been struck with earlier. Dazed, Elliot ceased his struggle. They dragged him into a room and put him on a stretcher. Once Elliot's arms and legs were tightly bound, the men exited the room, and Elliot took the opportunity to get a better look at where he was.

Bloody surgical instruments, pliers, and teeth lay on a tray beside him. He saw shelves with jars containing human body parts ranging from fingers and ears to a head and what looked like a penis.

One thing in particular that drew his attention was an oddly shaped black rock. Strange noises that sounded like whispers seemed to emanate from the rock, and Elliot could swear he could hear it calling to him. He couldn't tell if he was just hearing things. Perhaps it was his lack of sleep or food and water. Or maybe it was the pain of his wounds that had caused him to become delirious. Perhaps it was both? In any case, the strange rock continued to whisper in an indecipherable language.

The door to the room opened with a piercing whine of the iron hinges. A tall man with greasy brown hair and a scar on his cheek walked in, slamming the door shut behind him. He wore a faded white lab coat and a bloodstained apron. "Ah!" he exclaimed. "I'm glad you could make it to your appointment. Allow me to introduce myself: I am Doctor Meier. I run this ship. I trust your accommodations have been less than suitable. I would ask your name, but it's rather irrelevant to me." He sat down in a wheeled chair and rolled his way over to Elliot.

"What are you going to do to me?" asked Elliot.

"Oh, I have special plans for you, my boy," replied the doctor. "I have been traveling the world these past few years in search of the most toxic and *volatile* substances. I won't beat around the bush about it, so I'll be blunt with you. The end game of this whole operation is to develop a synthetic plague that will decimate the human population. And you, my irritating little friend, have the luxury of being my first guinea pig." The doctor pushed himself away from the stretcher and rolled over to his desk.

With the doctor's back turned, Elliot tried to break free from the restraints. It was no use. His captors had done their job well.

The doctor rolled back over to Elliot and placed some things onto the tray beside him. He got up from his chair and pulled a blanket off of some sort of machine, grabbed a pair of tongs, and opened a box on his desk. Using the tongs, the doctor pulled out a glass cylinder with an oddly colored green liquid inside and placed the cylinder into the machine.

Elliot had made a plan with Loki to take control of the ship, but being a guinea pig was not part of it. He hoped Loki would go through with the plan without him.

"I don't know about you, but I am very curious to see what happens," said the doctor as he set up a small camera on a tripod. "I hope you don't mind me recording this—purely for scientific purposes, of course." The doctor then rolled the stretcher into a room with a glass wall and positioned the stretcher vertically so Elliot could look out the glass.

"What the fuck is this?" pleaded Elliot.

"Oh, don't you worry; you'll see soon enough." The doctor exited the room, latching a steel door behind him.

"Why are you doing this? What's the point in destroying the world if *you're* still on it?"

From the other side of the glass, he spoke to Elliot. "Oh, my dear boy, my goal isn't to destroy the world. It's to *save* it."

"Maybe I just don't understand because I'm not a warped fuck like you."

"So naive," the doctor began. "Don't you see? The earth is sick, and I aim to cure it. Humans are such *disgusting* animals. We're no different than the apes we evolved from. Humans are a cancer, a virus, a parasite. We destroy everything we touch. I can't help but laugh at the young generation. To think that peace and equality are achievable in a society of narcissistic cretins. War and hatred are man's true instincts. The only way to save humanity is to destroy it." The doctor's words carried a deep sense of passion.

"And what exactly are you saving humanity from?" asked Elliot.

"Themselves," the doctor said coldly. "Shall we begin?" He flipped a switch on the machine, pressed a couple of buttons, and pulled down on a lever.

The machine made a hissing noise as it drained the liquid from the cylinder. A green cloud began pouring out from a vent above Elliot. He tried to hold his breath for as long as he could, but the green vapor began burning his eyes and skin, and he couldn't hold it any longer. "*Aahhhg!*" he screamed. The gas burned his mouth and throat as he breathed in. His heart began banging against his ribs as if it were trying to break out of his chest. His lungs burned like his insides were on fire. He coughed on the vapor, and blood began dripping from his mouth.

The doctor watched Elliot intently. "Remarkable!" he whispered to himself, scribbling his observations into a notebook.

Suddenly, a loud boom echoed throughout the ship, and the alarm siren sounded as the ship lurched to one side.

Caught off guard and curious as to what was going on, the doctor left the room and went out into the hall.

Elliot could see the red alarm lights flashing, but the sound of the siren was overpowered by the sound of blood pumping in his ears.

Another explosion somewhere on the ship caused the glass wall to shatter, allowing the vapor to escape and for Elliot to breathe. The ship lurched to the opposite side, and Elliot's stretcher fell to the floor along with everything else in the room.

Feeling around on the metal floor, Elliot pulled a shard of glass into his hand. The glass dug into his skin as he rubbed the edge of the shard against his restraints. He winced from the pain as blood trickled over his fingers, making the glass slippery and hard to hold on to. He pushed the shard deeper into his skin so he wouldn't lose his grip. Finally, he was able to free his left hand and undo the restraint on his right hand. He pulled the glass from his skin and wiped the blood on his pant leg. He tried to stand, but he could feel the chemicals coursing through his body. He collapsed to the floor in pain and exhaustion.

Another explosion rocked the ship, causing Elliot to roll across the floor.

The black rock rolled toward him. As he started to lose consciousness, Elliot could hear it talking to him in a language he couldn't understand. He watched the rock as a black fluid oozed its way out of a crack and slowly made its way toward him. The fluid seemed to have a mind of its own, wiggling its way onto Elliot's hand and dissolving into his open wound. He could feel a dark sensation wash over him. The blood in his veins turned black, and his skin turned pale. The voice from the rock grew louder and louder until it washed out the sound of blood pumping in his ears.

The doctor burst back into the room with a couple of guards. "Grab everything!" he ordered them.

Elliot grabbed the rock and tucked it under his side so it wouldn't be found. The two men worked quickly to grab as many documents as they could.

The doctor looked at Elliot and knelt down next to him. "It's regrettable that I can't stay and continue to watch you suffer. It's time I take off," he said. He straightened and turned. "Let's go. Take what you can to the helicopter on the landing pad," he told the guards.

Elliot could feel a strange sensation moving throughout his body. His vision faded in and out. The voice from the rock seemed to be echoing inside his head. Slowly, he lost consciousness.

Loki made her way to Elliot as fire began to overtake the ship. She found Elliot on the ground. She checked his pulse; it was faint, but it was there. After quickly hoisting Elliot onto her shoulders, Loki made her way out of the room. Fire blocked the path to the top deck on the right. She made a quick decision to go left and attempt to take the long route to the deck.

She raced down burning hallways with Elliot on her shoulders. Prisoners on the ship fought with guards and each other. Sounds of shots being fired echoed loudly. Canisters of gas and chemicals exploded from the heat, sending flames and fumes in every direction. Loki crossed the holding block and headed up a stairwell. The smoke grew heavy and thick. She dropped to her knees and laid Elliot down on his back. She crawled on the floor under the smoke, dragging Elliot behind her. The progress was slow, but she was determined. She reached a closed door. Only one more hallway and flight of stairs until she and Elliot were safely on the top deck. She grabbed the lock on the door, but it wouldn't budge. She hit the lock and laid into it with all her weight.

Prisoners who were trying to escape the fire came running up the hallway. A large man from Loki's tribe grabbed the wheel on the door and twisted it with all his might until it gave in, and the door opened.

Pipes were bursting from the heat, sending scalding water and steam in every direction. Burning debris fell all around them. The large tribal man picked up Elliot, tucked him under his arm, and ran down the hallway.

"We have to get topside, quick!" yelled Loki.

A guard opened a door in front of them. With his free hand, the man carrying Elliot grabbed the guard by his head and slammed him into a pipe on the wall. "Let's go!" he commanded, giving a wave to Loki and the others.

They ascended the final staircase and made it to the top deck. Prisoners who had gotten ahold of weapons were fighting the guards and trying to run them overboard.

Loki pointed to a small boat chained to the side of the ship. "There!"

The ship exploded before Loki, Elliot, and the others could make it off. A large plume of flames and smoke stretched toward the sky. Chunks of metal and other debris rained down into the ocean. The burning hull of the ship slowly sank into the depths of the ocean as sharks made their way inward, picking off any survivors floating in the water. Their bodies, among many others, sank into the depths of the ocean.

The doctor could see the large cloud of smoke from several miles away in his helicopter. In his hand, he held a detonator.

"What's the plan now?" A man with an eyepatch asked the doctor.

"We'll have to start again, but at least I have my research," the doctor replied coldly. "The scum of this earth doesn't know it, but their days are numbered."

"Where to, sir?" asked the pilot over the radio.

"Sterling City," the doctor replied. "There is much work to be done."

CHAPTER 1

THE BODY

Sixty-three miles off the coast of Sterling City, a pair of fishermen had found Elliot's body tangled in their fishing net.

"Dad! Come quick!" the younger of the two men called out. He pointed to the corpse among the fish.

The two men cut the net around the body. Once it was freed from the net, they covered it with a sheet and quickly made their way back to shore.

It was around nine-thirty at night when Commissioner James Lowell arrived at the marina. For Commissioner Lowell, a body in Sterling City was nothing out of the ordinary. The city was riddled with crime, and having grown up on the west side, he was more than accustomed to it.

Lowell greeted the two fishermen and two officers who were already at the scene.

"We were finishing up for the day and were pulling our net up when we found it tangled in with some fish," the older of the two fishermen said.

"The body is right over here if you would like to take a look, sir," one of the policemen said.

The policeman escorted Lowell to where the body had been laid on the dock, the dirty sheet still covering it. Lowell stooped down and pulled the edge of the sheet down past the head. The skin and muscle had been stripped from the bone, leaving the skull completely exposed. Lowell grimaced and pulled the sheet back over the head. "Any identification?" he asked the police officer.

"None, sir."

"Wonderful. Get this body to the morgue. Let's see if we can get some ID and a cause of death."

The body lay motionless on the table. It was less of a body and more of something you would see in a horror film. There was no skin or flesh on the head or neck. The torso was mangled by burns, cuts, and scars. Torn pieces of flesh left parts of the rib cage exposed. The right hand was completely stripped of flesh up to the mid forearm, and the left hand was charred.

A spectacled older gentleman in a white lab coat sat beside the examination table, closely observing all the injuries and taking notes on a pad next to him.

Commissioner Lowell entered the room. The lab door slamming behind him caught the old man off guard.

"Ah, James! How nice of you to stop by. I was just getting ready for bed when I got your call," said the old man.

"This isn't how I wanted to spend my night either. Got anything for me?"

"Well …" the old man began. "What really caught my attention was the skull."

Lowell moved in to get a better look.

"You see how all the skin and flesh are gone? There's no tearing or burns here at the edge of the skin. It's almost like it receded on its own or simply melted as though it were wax."

"Can you determine a cause of death?"

"I was just going to enter my notes into my computer and get started on that when you walked in here. There are no indications on the exterior of the body that hint at a cause of death. An autopsy will have to be performed to find a cause. If you would like to stick around, I could always use an extra pair of hands."

"I'm all set. I'll stick to the investigations in the streets."

"Suit yourself," the old man chuckled. "Good night, James."

As Lowell left, the doctor went to his computer and sat down at his desk, back turned to the exam table. He began entering his notes into his computer, clacking away at the keyboard. He was so focused on his work, he didn't notice the lights in the room flickering.

The light above the exam table flickered aggressively, and the room got cold. Slowly, Elliot's body sat upright on the table. He swung his legs to the side and sat on the edge. Using his bony right hand, he rubbed his skinless face. He got to his feet and slowly staggered toward the door.

The doctor heard the noise behind him and turned around in time to see the corpse standing in the doorway. He removed his glasses, rubbed the lenses on his coat, and put them back on his face. Convinced he wasn't just seeing things, he opened a drawer in his desk and pulled out a short revolver. The doctor stood up and aimed his weapon. His hands shook nervously as he lined up the sights and fired two shots into Elliot's back.

Elliot felt a dark energy wash over him; he was not himself. Under the control of an otherworldly influence, he turned around to face the doctor. It was almost like he was being possessed.

The doctor, frightened, fired another two shots, this time, right into Elliot's chest.

Unfazed by the bullets, Elliot started toward his aggressor in a threatening manner.

The doctor fired his last two shots and continued pulling the trigger, unaware of the empty clicks the gun was making.

Elliot approached the man and with his bony hand, grabbed him by the throat and hoisted him into the air, pinning him to the wall.

The doctor struggled to break free from the grasp, kicking and swinging his fists, even hitting Elliot in the skull with the gun.

Elliot took the pistol with his other hand and threw it across the room. Tightening his grip, he began to choke the man.

As the man gasped for air, his skin began to turn pale and whither. His hair grew long and white. His eyes sank deep into his skull. "Wh-what are you?" he choked out.

As the doctor's energy was drained from him, the skin on Elliot's right hand started to grow back on his fingertips. It grew up his hand and reconnected seamlessly with the skin on his forearm. The burns and cuts on his chest healed, leaving no visible marks behind. The skin around his shoulders began to grow and crawl its way up his neck, tendons and muscles forming around the bone as the skin quickly covered it. Long and scraggly jet-black hair sprouted from his head and grew to his shoulders.

An unkempt beard grew over his face. He opened his eyelids to reveal piercing gray eyes that stared right into the doctor's.

Elliot leaned in close to the man's ear. "Death," he whispered, dropping the man's lifeless body onto the floor in a crumpled heap.

Elliot took a few steps backward and staggered. He fell to the floor, watching as the room seemed to spin around him. Regaining some sense of normalcy, he looked at the withered body on the floor. Startled by the sight, he gasped and pushed himself away from it. "What the fuck?" he said to himself. His breathing was heavy. "I need to get out of here."

Elliot pulled himself up to his feet. Holding on to the wall, he made his way to the door and let himself out into a long corridor. A sign to his right indicated the direction of the exit. Still holding on to the wall, he shuffled his way down the corridor.

"Hey, you! Stop!" called out a voice from behind Elliot.

Elliot turned and saw a uniformed security guard making his way toward him.

The man shined a bright light into Elliot's eyes. "Who are you?" he asked.

Elliot didn't move or respond.

"Who. Are. You?" the security guard asked again.

Elliot could feel that same dark energy begin to wash over him again as his veins turned from blue to black.

As the security guard grabbed Elliot by the shoulder, Elliot put his hand to the man's chest. A black, shadowy force surged from Elliot's hand, sending the man flying backward down the corridor and into a brick wall. The security guard didn't move.

Elliot fell to his hands and knees, feeling drained as the dark energy left him. At this time, Elliot realized he wasn't wearing any clothes. He looked up the hall and saw the security guard's body still crumpled on the floor. Next to him was a door leading to a locker room.

As Elliot was entering the locker room, he looked at the man's body. His skin was pale, and his eyes were sunken, a look of painful terror on his face.

Elliot found some scrub pants and a pair of sneakers that just barely fit. He found a "Sterling City Hockey" hoodie and put that on. He braced himself on the sides of a sink and looked into the mirror. It was a face he barely recognized. He blinked as he saw the reflection of a grizzly-looking skeleton staring back at him. Startled, he stepped back from the sink and then turned on the faucet and splashed cold water onto his face. When he looked back at the mirror, the skeleton was gone. Making his way to the exit, Elliot paid no attention to the body crumpled outside the locker room. When he got to the exit, he pulled the hood down over his face and stepped outside into the streets.

Outside in the streets of the city, Elliot knew exactly where he was. Sterling City was his home; he grew up there. *What the fuck?* he thought to himself. Elliot hadn't been home in more than three years. The last thing Elliot remembered was being on a prison ship in the middle of some God-forsaken ocean.

He walked slowly down the sidewalk, looking around at all the sights around him. *How did I get here?* he wondered. Elliot was oblivious to the fact that he had just stepped into the street.

A car hit its brakes and screeched as it came toward Elliot, and the driver slammed on his horn.

Blinded and bracing for impact, Elliot raised his arms, holding his hands in front of his face. As the car screeched closer, Elliot could feel the dark energy wash over him once again. The energy manifested itself from Elliot's hands into a black mass that flew straight into the vehicle, stopping it dead in its tracks. The front of the car was smashed in, and all of the windows were shattered. Adrenaline surged through Elliot's body. "What did I do?" he asked himself.

Elliot quickly turned and looked to see if anyone had witnessed what had just happened, but he was alone in the streets. Nervously, he made his way to the driver's side of the car. The driver was an old man. He was slumped against the steering wheel. A gash on the man's head trickled with blood. Elliot extended a shaky hand to the man's neck, checking for a pulse. The airbags had deployed, but they did no good; the man was dead.

Elliot tugged on the drawstrings of his hoodie, pulling the hood tighter around his face. He ran as quickly as he could away from the car. As he ran, he kept replaying the scenes at the morgue in his head. Had he really killed those two men? And now a third? *This* has *to be a dream*, he thought to himself. *A nightmare.*

Elliot walked and walked. He kept his hands in his pockets and his head hung low. He tried to make sense of everything, but he just couldn't. He thought back to the prison ship. Perhaps this was a side effect of whatever the doctor had done to him? *Am I hallucinating? Am I dead?* he thought to himself.

Elliot was so focused on his thoughts that he didn't notice shrubs and plants withering and dying as he walked past them.

Elliot looked at everything around him, trying to take it all in. He recognized everything but still felt lost. He felt like he was in his own world. He could see everything around him, but he didn't feel like he was really there; he didn't feel in the present. All of this felt like some sort of weird out-of-body experience. "Maybe I really am dead." Elliot contemplated it.

Earlier …

"All units, we have reports of a car accident on the corner of Cliff and Stellar just outside the city morgue. Reports of shots being fired. Suspect unknown, proceed with caution," came a voice over a police radio.

A man walked to the radio and turned it off. He stepped out of his front door and closed it behind him. Under the darkness of night and the light of the moon, a pitch-black smoke washed over the man. The smoke rolled down from his head, covering it with a black cowl. As the smoke rolled down his shoulders and torso, it dressed him in a long, black, tattered cloak and a burgundy tunic with a black vest over it. The man turned his head to the sky. The moonlight shone on him and revealed that the black smoke had taken all the flesh from his bones, leaving a haunting skeleton behind. Darkness swirled around him, and he disappeared into the night.

A dark, smoky cloud formed outside the morgue, and the cloaked skeleton seemed to materialize inside it. He stepped onto the pavement of the sidewalk. The dark cloud dissipated into the air.

The skeleton looked around for any signs of police. He had arrived before they did. He silently glided over the pavement toward the totaled car. He looked closely at the dead man inside. Moving away from the car, he glided toward the morgue. Not opening the doors, he simply went straight through them as if they weren't there.

He looked down the hallway of the morgue and saw the security guard slumped against the wall. In a ghostly manner, he glided down the hall and observed the corpse. He moved away and materialized through the wall of the security room.

He looked at the security monitors. Reaching out with a bony hand, he tapped a couple of keys on the keyboard. He rewound the security footage to earlier. He pressed a key, and the footage began to play.

He watched the footage as Elliot's body rose up off the exam table. He observed how Elliot had drained the man's life essence and healed his own wounds. Elliot turned toward the camera. The skeleton paused the footage. He now had a face to look for. He clicked and zoomed in on the footage. There were strange scars on Elliot's chest that formed some sort of symbol.

"Hmm." The skeleton waved his hand over the electronics. All the screens on the monitor turned black. He corrupted the security hard drives, so the police wouldn't be able to view it. Then just as before, he vanished into thin air.

The skeleton materialized outside. He could hear sirens in the distance, getting closer by the second. He quickly made his way from the area, gliding over the pavement and scanning for any evidence that might indicate where Elliot had gone.

As he made his way down the streets, he came across some dead and withered plants. The dead plants seemed out of place. Other plants in the area seemed perfectly healthy. He knew he was on Elliot's trail. Once again, the skeleton vanished into the night in a cloud of black smoke.

As Elliot made his way down Beverly Street, a man stepped out of an alley behind him. Elliot glanced over his shoulder and saw the man following him. Elliot slowly picked up his pace. The man behind Elliot sped up as well. Elliot couldn't make out who it was.

As Elliot tried to get away from the man following him, two more men stepped out from an alley and cut him off.

"Where you off to in a hurry at this time of night?" one growled.

Elliot turned around to run the other way, but the man behind him struck him in the head with a blunt object and knocked him to the ground.

"Search him. Grab anything he has," said one of the men.

The man who hit him knelt down beside Elliot and started frisking him. "He doesn't have anything."

Elliot hit the man in the groin and tried to stand up but was kicked in the head by the other man. Dazed, Elliot fell back to the ground. He saw the man moving in on him and watched as he raised his foot above his head. Elliot closed his eyes and braced himself.

A heavy wind rushed over Elliot, and he heard the men grunt as if they had been struck by something. Elliot opened his eyes and watched as two of the men made their way toward a hooded figure. A black wind seemed to materialize from nowhere and strike both the men, sending them flying backward.

The two men climbed to their feet and faced their attacker.

"Fuck! It's the Reaper!" yelled the man who followed Elliot.

"Let's get him!" said the other man, pulling a large knife from his belt. "I've heard stories about you. Wouldn't you be a nice prize?" he said to the hooded figure standing in the street.

"The Reaper," they had called him. He had heard many names. He stood in the open street, his face silhouetted by his hood. Black smoke clung to his robes and danced subtly in the breeze, making him appear phantom-like. The black smoke rolled down his robes and pooled on the ground at his feet. He ignored Elliot's presence for the moment and focused his attention on the two men. He stood quietly, waiting for them to make the first move.

The man who drew the knife ran at the Reaper, raising his arm into the air to prepare for a strike.

The Reaper waited. When the man was steps away, the Reaper drew a black-bladed sword from his robes. With one quick and fluid swing, the Reaper cut off the man's arm. The Reaper stepped aside as the man moved past him, and he followed his first swing with a second one that split the man in half at the waist.

The body parts fell to the ground without a single drop of blood being spilled.

The Reaper turned and faced the second man. He sheathed his sword and waited.

The second man, not being someone to bring a knife to a sword fight, pulled out a pistol and aimed it at the Reaper. He tried to pull the trigger, but he couldn't. A dark fear and panic took hold of the man and paralyzed him. He couldn't move a muscle; he was like a deer in the headlights, a deer with a gun.

The Reaper slowly approached the man.

The fear in the man grew more intense with each step the Reaper took toward him, but he still could not move.

The Reaper stood in front of the gun. He stuck out his bony right hand, mimicking a gun, and pointed it at the man. Slowly, the Reaper moved his hand toward himself and pointed his finger gun at his own head.

Possessed by the fear of the Reaper, the man pointed the gun to his head against his will.

The man began to sob like a baby.

The Reaper looked at the man. "Tell me, do you feel dead?" he asked him.

As the Reaper curled his finger in, the man pulled the trigger on the gun, sending brains and blood onto the pavement. The man's body fell to the ground as blood pooled around him.

The third thug turned and tried to escape as fast as he could, but he was too slow for the Reaper.

The Reaper extended his left hand and used his powers to yank the man backward through the air, only to be met with the black blade that pierced his back and protruded through his chest. Flesh began to sizzle and burn from the heat of the blade.

Elliot, who had just witnessed all of this, was fairly certain he had shit himself. He crawled into the alley and leaned against the brick side of a building. He put a hand to his head; he could feel the wound on his head, but there was no blood.

The Reaper glided toward Elliot.

Elliot looked at him, trying to figure out who it was, but he was silhouetted. "Don't kill me, please!" he pleaded.

"Who are you?" the Reaper asked.

"What?" asked Elliot.

The Reaper drew his black sword and swung it at Elliot's head, stopping just before he made contact with his neck.

Elliot could feel an intense heat emanating from the blade as if it were red hot.

The Reaper repeated his question. "Who are you? *Don't* make me ask you again."

"I-I'm … my name is Elliot. What do you want?"

"I want to know who the fuck you are and why you've been leaving a trail of bodies all over the city!" the Reaper demanded.

"I … it's not me … I swear," said Elliot. In his defense, he really didn't feel like he was himself.

The Reaper stuck his other hand out.

Some sort of unseen force picked Elliot off the ground and pinned him against the wall behind him.

The Reaper used his sword and removed a chunk of Elliot's hoodie, showing the strangely shaped scar on his chest. "Where did you get this?" the Reaper asked.

"I-I don't remember," replied Elliot. "I don't remember a thing. I don't even know how I got here!" he pleaded.

The Reaper could sense that Elliot was telling the truth and had no memory of where he was or how he got there. He lowered Elliot to his feet.

"Are you going to kill me?"

"Not right now anyway. You really don't remember anything?"

"I swear! I don't remember a thing. I just woke up in a morgue, and I barely remember that."

"Ah, so you're the body that washed up on shore."

"How do you know that?"

The Reaper sheathed his sword and pulled out a police radio, showed it to Elliot, and then put it back under his cloak. "I've been monitoring the police in the city."

"Are you a cop?"

"After all that? What the fuck do you think?"

"I already told you, I don't know. I honestly don't know what to think right now. Nothing seems real."

"Leave and never show your face around here again," the Reaper said coldly.

Elliot's breaths shook with nervousness. "What?" he asked. "Can't you help me?" he asked the Reaper.

"No. Now leave," the Reaper replied.

"Please, please help me. I'll do anything."

The Reaper stood still and quiet, like he was thinking about something. "Why?" he asked.

"If you won't help me, then just kill me," said Elliot, bowing his head.

"Come with me."

"Where are we going?"

"Do you want to get your memory back?"

"You're gonna help me?"

"Would you rather I kill you instead?"

Elliot wasn't sure he trusted the Reaper, but he also wasn't sure that he had much of a choice. "Lead the way."

"Hold on to my cloak," said the Reaper, extending his arm toward Elliot.

"Why?" asked Elliot, hesitantly reaching forward.

"Just do it."

Elliot took ahold of the Reaper's cloak, and a thick black smoke began to swirl up from their feet and devoured the two of them.

CHAPTER 2

WHO IS ELLIOT BLYTHE?

The Reaper had taken Elliot to a heavily forested part of Sterling City. Following the Reaper down the dark path in silence, Elliot could feel the cool autumn air rolling through the trees. He looked up at the bare branches silhouetted against the full moon.

Elliot listened for any signs of life in the forest, but the only sound came from his own footsteps. He looked up at the Reaper ahead of him, gliding silently and smoothly over the gravel path. Wondering where exactly he was being taken, Elliot decided to break the silence. "Gonna tell me where we're going yet?" he asked.

"I told you, we're going to get your memories back," the Reaper replied. "And if I'm feeling nice, maybe I'll even help with your little Reaper problem," he added.

"What do you mean?" Elliot asked.

The Reaper stopped moving and turned to Elliot, the moon baring light on his skull. "Well, to put it bluntly, you're just like me, buddy."

Elliot stopped walking. He felt panic and anxiety wash over him. "Am … am I dead?"

"In a way, yes," said the Reaper. "But the Reaper inside you is keeping you alive. It's a kind of symbiotic relationship. You take care of it, and it'll take care of you," he explained. "Once you learn to control it, you can *reap* the benefits."

"Jesus fucking Christ," said Elliot. "How long have you been sitting on that one?"

The Reaper forced an exhale. "Long enough," he replied. "Why don't we wait on the questions for now?"

As they continued walking, the woods around them became eerily quiet. Even the wind seemed to stop. Far ahead on the trail, Elliot could see the faint yellow glow of a light. Feeling uncomfortable in the eerie silence, he decided to break it again. "So, you're the Reaper," he said. "I used to hear stories about you when I was a kid. Never actually thought you were real though."

"I prefer it that way," replied the Reaper.

"I never got your name," said Elliot.

"And?" the Reaper replied passively.

"Well, what is it?" prodded Elliot.

"It's Valentine," he said shortly.

"Valentine? Like the day?" asked Elliot. "How adorable," he said sarcastically.

"Killing you is still an option, in case you were wondering."

They came to a small cabin in the woods with burning candles in the window. Valentine knocked on the door with his bony hand.

The door swung open as if it were being opened by a gorilla. But instead, they were greeted by a small old woman with gray curls spiraling in all directions. An emerald-green cloth wrapped around her head and covered her eyes. A purple shawl wrapped around her shoulders and draped to the floor. "Ah, Valentine, my dear. Come in! Come in! How are you, now?" she said with a grandmotherly softness.

"I'm doing just fine, busy as usual. How are you? Keeping out of trouble, I hope," replied Valentine.

The old lady chuckled.

Elliot followed Valentine into the woman's cabin. The walls were lined with all kinds of oddities, ranging from animal and human skulls to colorful powders, more burning candles, feathers, strange paintings, and a taxidermied beaver with a top hat. Stacks of books filled whatever space was left in the room. Sage hung from the rafters, and the room smelled of strong incense.

The old lady made her way to a burning fireplace. "May I get you boys a hot drink? Batwing tea perhaps?" the old lady offered hospitably.

"I think we're all right for now," Valentine politely declined. "Misha, I was wondering if you could help my acquaintance here?"

The old lady walked to Elliot and tilted her head at him, almost as if she could see through the blindfold. "Yes, sit. Of course I can help," she said to Valentine. "You two take a seat."

Elliot and Valentine took a seat at a wooden table with bat wings and other small animal parts scattered across it. Elliot tried not to make it obvious he was grossed out.

The old lady climbed onto a seat across from the two. "What can I help you with, my dear?"

"My friend here is a Reaper, but he's detached from it," Valentine explained. "On top of that, he's lost all memory."

"Mmmm. Quite the predicament you've got there, yes?" asked Misha, pointing her head toward Elliot.

"Please, if you can help me, I'll do anything," Elliot pleaded.

"Anything, hmmm?" Misha chuckled. "I require no payment. I am always glad to assist Valentine." Misha hopped down from her seat. Moving gracefully and with intent, she made her way around the cluttered room and began rummaging through drawers and boxes, tossing things around and putting the odd item into one of her pockets.

Elliot leaned into Valentine. "Is she blind?" he whispered.

"One doesn't need eyes to see, my dear. Just like one doesn't need ears to *listen*," said Misha from across the room. She put something black into a bowl and ground it into a fine powder before pouring it into a small bag. She then gave the powder and the contents of her pockets to Valentine. "This should be all you need."

"Thank you," replied Valentine, putting everything inside his cloak. "You're a saint from the heavens, Misha."

"You are like a son to me," she said fondly, putting a small hand on Valentine's arm. "If you ever need anything, just ask."

Valentine nudged Elliot and nodded his head toward Misha.

"Yes! Thank you so much," said Elliot. "I really appreciate this."

"You do as he tells you, yes?" said Misha.

"I will," he replied.

Valentine and Elliot exited the cabin and stepped outside.

"I know it should be cold out," said Elliot. "But how come I don't feel anything?" he asked.

"One of the benefits of the Reaper," replied Valentine. "Protects you from the elements. Won't get too hot or too cold."

"So what now?" asked Elliot.

"Grab my cloak."

"I really don't care for this," said Elliot. "It makes me nauseous."

"Do it," Valentine ordered.

Elliot grabbed the sleeve of Valentine's cloak, and once again, the black smoke swirled around and devoured them.

When the smoke cleared, they were in a room with a cobblestone floor. Large pillars stretching to the ceiling formed a circle around them. Flaming torches attached to the pillars lit up the room.

"Where are we?" asked Elliot.

"My meditation chamber," replied Valentine.

"How do you do the smoky teleport thing?"

"You ask too many questions," said Valentine. "The Reaper allows you to travel through darkness." He paused for a moment. "But you have to know where you're going. Otherwise, traveling through the darkness can be a trip," he added.

Valentine lit a small fire between him and Elliot. "Take a seat," he said, pointing to the floor.

Elliot and Valentine sat down across from each other.

Valentine took the powder and vials that Misha had given him, poured them into a bowl, and mixed them.

"So how exactly do I get my memory back?" asked Elliot.

"Well," said Valentine, focusing on the bowl, "won't be fun. Well, not for *you* anyway."

"What do you mean?" said Elliot, concerned. "Have you done this before?" he asked.

"Nope!" said Valentine. "Which is the fun part," he added, sounding excited.

When the contents of the bowl were mixed, Valentine set the bowl on the coals of the fire.

"See, now, the way you're talking makes me not wanna do this." Elliot was starting to have second thoughts about the whole thing, but on the other hand, he wasn't sure he had much of a choice.

"Relax!" said Valentine. "What's the worst that'll happen? You'll *die?*" he asked sarcastically. "You'll be fine." Valentine removed the bowl from the coals and handed it to Elliot. "Here, drink this."

Elliot took the cup and looked inside. The black liquid bubbled and moved like it was alive, and it smelled like rotting flesh. Elliot grimaced and tried not to throw up. "Do I really have to drink this?" he asked.

"Yes!" Valentine replied sternly.

Elliot hesitantly put the bowl to his lips and tipped it back. He took a bigger sip than he intended and almost threw up. He could feel the gross concoction crawling its way down his throat. "God! What the fuck is this stuff?" asked Elliot, gagging.

Valentine shrugged. "Buckle up, amigo."

Valentine's words sounded distorted to him, and the room began to swirl and spin around him. Darkness began to creep up on him, and both Valentine and the fire disappeared from sight. Elliot felt like he was going to pass out as everything turned to black.

All of a sudden, Elliot felt like he was being ripped downward, falling through the darkness. He screamed and flailed his arms and legs as he fell. As he kept falling, he could see a small light ahead of him, growing larger and larger the longer he fell.

The light opened to a wide sky with an ocean down below. Elliot could feel the wind and moisture of the air rush past him with a deafening noise. "Fuck, fuck, fuck!" he yelled, speeding toward the surface of the water.

The water slapped him as he breached the surface. Elliot sank into the water. He struggled to swim upward as he gasped for air, but it felt as though something was dragging him down deeper. He kept gasping for air, but his lungs filled with water. As he started to pass out, Elliot could feel the water rush over him as if it were all being drained out. The surface of the water grew closer and closer.

Elliot washed up onto a sandy beach. Turning onto his hands and knees, he coughed up sea water and filled his lungs with fresh air. He looked around him; the beach and foliage ahead of him all seemed familiar, but he couldn't remember where he had seen it all before.

Elliot could see someone in the distance walking toward him.

It was a young girl, wearing a bright-blue dress and a wide white sunhat, walking barefoot in the sand. "You're not supposed to be here," she said when she reached Elliot.

"What? Who-who are you?" asked Elliot.

"You shouldn't be here," repeated the girl.

"Wh-where *should* I be?" Elliot was still trying to catch his breath.

The girl pointed up the beach to a thick black cloud floating above the sand. "Go. It will show you."

"*It?*" asked Elliot, confused. He looked at the black mass lingering in the air.

"Elliot …" came a whisper. "Elliot …" The voice seemed to be coming from the dark cloud.

"Go," repeated the girl softly.

Elliot struggled to his feet and stumbled toward the cloud.

"Elliot … Elliot …" it called.

As Elliot got closer to the black cloud, it floated gently away from him, leading Elliot on a path up a small hill. Elliot continued to follow it.

The cloud sped up the hill, and as it reached the top, it took the shape of a robed figure.

"Who?" Elliot began to ask himself. As he reached the top of the hill, Elliot could see the figure dressed in a black cloak. "Valentine?" he asked.

The figure had its back to Elliot and was overlooking a freshly dug grave with a marbled headstone at the front of it.

"He … hello?" asked Elliot.

The only noise the figure made was a soft, muffled cry.

"Hello?" Elliot asked again, reaching forward to touch the person on the shoulder.

Before his hand touched the cloak, the person spun around.

Elliot gasped in horror and almost stumbled backward.

The cloaked figure was … *himself.*

Elliot peered around the side of the ghostly apparition of himself and saw his own name carved into the headstone.

Before Elliot could react, the apparition grabbed him and pulled him forward. Elliot could feel the coldness of the apparition as the black smoke washed over him, and he stumbled into the open grave. There was no bottom to the grave, so Elliot kept falling and falling until once again, he was consumed by darkness.

There was an abrupt stop when Elliot finally hit the bottom of the grave. He felt as though he had fallen miles.

Torches began to light on their own, one at a time, revealing an underground tunnel.

Elliot staggered to his feet and clung to the wall to keep himself up. He began shuffling his way down the tunnel. As he slowly moved down the tunnel, he could hear voices up ahead, jumbled murmurs. As he got even closer, the murmurs began to sound clearer and more rhythmic.

The tunnel opened to a small room that was well lit by torches. A group of robed and hooded people with their backs turned to Elliot sang a hymn in a foreign language. As Elliot entered the room, without stopping their singing, the people slowly turned to him, smiled at him, and cleared a path to the front of the room where another man stood. The people behind him closed the path as he moved forward.

The man in the front stood in a waist-high pool of a black liquid. He stood with his back to Elliot, facing toward a statue of a black-winged woman with skeletons crawling at her feet. She held a black stone in one hand and a human skull in the other.

As Elliot approached the pool, the man turned around to face him.

The man raised his hand in the air, and the crowd stopped singing their hymn. He addressed the hooded people. "Children," he started. "Today a stranger is among us!" He looked at Elliot. "Tell us, stranger, what have you come for? I sense that you are lost and are looking for something."

"Y-yes?" said Elliot.

"Do you seek to know your *true* self? To unlock the inner sanctums of your being?" the man asked Elliot.

"Yes."

"Come forth, my son, and together, we shall unite your physical form with the entity within. Together, we can awaken your true self. Do you accept the will of the Mother of Death, our guardian who watches over lost souls?" he asked, raising a hand toward the statue.

Elliot could feel a heavy weight on his chest, and his breath was short. "Yes," he replied.

"Then come forward now and accept your *true* self. Accept your new life as one of our Mother's creations," the old man said, extending a hand to Elliot.

As Elliot stepped into the black pool, the audience of robed people moved in closer.

The old man spoke to Elliot, turning him to face the crowd. "Do you accept the Reaper within you? Will you vow to serve the Mother's will?" He put his hand on Elliot's shoulder.

"Yes," said Elliot.

"Will you accept the baptism of the Reaper?"

"Yes."

The old man folded Elliot's arms across his chest and leaned him backward.

Elliot could feel the black liquid wash over him and sear his skin. Elliot was lifted from the water, but before he could yell from the pain, a black-bladed knife was thrust into his chest by one of the members of the crowd. He could feel himself slip into the darkness as he sank to the bottom of the pool.

Feeling the blade puncture his heart, Elliot sat upward quickly and clasped his hands to his chest, but the knife wasn't there. He looked up and saw Valentine sitting across from him, meditating.

"Hmm, you're alive," said Valentine, sounding somewhat surprised.

Elliot was shaking and sweating. He rolled onto his hands and knees to catch his breath.

"Well?" said Valentine. "How do you feel?" he asked.

Elliot nodded his head, struggling to find the words—and his breath. "Is this real?" he finally managed to ask while rubbing his eyes with the palms of his hands. "It was … weird. Like a bad trip."

"Do you remember anything?" asked Valentine. "Your *name* for example."

Elliot wiped his hands down his face. "It's Elliot," he replied. "Elliot Blythe."

"Good, we're getting somewhere!" Valentine exclaimed. "Anything else?" he asked.

"I-I remember being on a ship," replied Elliot.

"What kind of ship?" asked Valentine.

"Some … sort of prison ship. I remember it exploding."

"Well, that would explain why they found your body in the ocean," said Valentine. "You remember anything about the black mark on your chest?"

Elliot put his hand on his chest and rubbed the scar. "I remember … some kind of … black rock, I think. I still feel pretty fuzzy right now."

Valentine took a rolled paper from his cloak, put it to his skull, and lit the end of it, taking a long drag from it. "That mark on your chest is the sign of the Reaper. The rock you mentioned sounds like a relic of Black Death." He handed it to Elliot.

"What is that?" asked Elliot.

"It's called malice. Should help you feel a bit better."

"No, thanks," replied Elliot. "So, do you mean, like, the plague?"

"The Black Death was the first Reaper, an ancient, powerful entity that aimed to wipe out the living and make an army of the dead. Countless times, people released him from the depths of the darkness so he could wreak havoc. Wars, plagues, famines—all because of the Black Death."

"So, what about the relics?" Elliot asked.

"After the Second World War, Black Death was defeated, and his being was split into several small pieces, called relics. The relic grants an individual immense power, but they can easily fall to the darkness that dwells within them."

"Is that how you became a Reaper?" inquired Elliot.

Valentine sighed. "No, but that's a story for another time."

Elliot had a lot on his mind. Remembering three years' of memories was making him feel woozy. He remembered his girlfriend, if she still *was* his girlfriend. He remembered his brother, Matthew, and his foster sister Rebecca. "I, uh … I think I need some fresh air." His head was swirling with thoughts and memories. "I-I'm gonna get going," he said, struggling to stand up.

"Going where?" asked Valentine.

"I-I dunno," replied Elliot.

"Going to be all right?" asked Valentine.

"Yeah." Elliot started to feel a little better now that he was on his feet. "How, um, how exactly do I get back to the city?" he asked.

"Easy!" exclaimed Valentine. "Meet me at this address tomorrow night," he said, handing Elliot a piece of paper with an address written on it. Valentine stood and extended his hands. "All right, picture where you want to go."

"My old apart—"

"You don't need to say it." Valentine interrupted. "Just picture it, and focus. Got it?"

"Yeah," Elliot replied.

"Ready?" asked Valentine.

Elliot nodded.

Thick plumes of black smoke poured from the tips of Valentine's fingers.

Elliot watched as the smoke wrapped around his ankles and climbed his legs and torso until he was completely consumed and blinded by it.

The smoke fell to the floor and dissipated into the air, and Elliot was gone.

Elliot walked through a space that was completely devoid of light and life. He moved along through the space feeling like he was being guided by a pair of unseen hands. Far ahead in the blackness, he could see a thin sliver of light breaking through the dark. Elliot approached the sliver of light and peered through it.

On the other side of the darkness, Elliot could see the wall of a brick building and a dumpster, dimly lit by a streetlight several yards away.

Elliot stepped through the sliver and into a dark alleyway. He walked to the street to his left and looked up at the green street sign labeled "Beacon St." Elliot looked up and down the street. "It worked," he said to himself.

Beacon Street was the host of his duplex apartment that he had rented with his girlfriend, May, three years prior.

Elliot struggled to process everything that had happened that night as he walked to his old apartment. Memories were coming back to him in little bits and chunks. Coming up to his old apartment and looking up at the door, he wiped his face with his hand and let out a sigh. He was nervous, and his heart was beating like it was going to jump right out of his chest.

He walked down the stone pathway and up the three concrete steps that led to his old door. He knocked a few times and waited for an answer. With no answer at the door, he then rang the doorbell twice. He could hear a muffled voice coming from somewhere behind the door.

The door opened, and very tall and muscular man with no neck, wearing a tank top and boxers, stood in the doorway. Even though half asleep, he still looked like he could crush a person's head between his hands. Elliot recognized him as a guy who frequented the gym that May worked at.

"What do you want?" asked the menacing man in a deep voice.

"Babe, who is it?" came May's voice from somewhere in the house.

Elliot knew it was her; he was *sure* of it. He could recognize her beautiful voice anywhere. Looking at the man in the doorway, Elliot started to panic. "Uh-uhh, I think I have the wrong address," Elliot said quickly before running down the steps and pathway and down the street out of sight.

After running for a block or so, Elliot stopped and looked behind him to make sure he wasn't being followed. When he was sure the large man wasn't chasing after him, Elliot walked over to a bench facing the street and sat down. He rested his head on his knees and tucked his arms in around his head. He was already having trouble processing everything that had happened that night, and finding out his girlfriend had moved on was only complicating things.

May was the only thing that had given Elliot the strength to survive for three years on a remote island. Carrying a small picture of May with him while on the island gave him what he needed to push on and find his way back to Sterling City.

Elliot didn't know what to do now; he felt lost. Picking his head up and sitting straight, he remembered his foster sister, Rebecca. Elliot hoped she still had her apartment on Silver Street. Without any money to buy a bus ride ten blocks, Elliot had no choice but to walk the whole way.

Elliot and Rebecca had met years ago when they were kids. They had both been placed into the same foster home where they were physically and mentally abused for years until they were both adopted by a much nicer family. Having endured so much together for so many years, they developed a sibling-like bond with each other and remained close friends even after they had both left their adoptive home.

After what seemed like hours, Elliot finally reached Rebecca's apartment building. He went in the front door and entered the lobby. He checked the registry by the mailboxes.

Rebecca Stewart. Rm. 311

"She's still here!" Elliot said to himself, sighing in relief. He took the elevator up to the third floor and walked down to the end of the hall. *Room three-eleven*, he thought to himself. He knocked on the door and waited.

There was no response.

Elliot knocked on the door again and waited. He could feel the presence of someone behind the door, looking at him through the peephole.

"Bex?" Elliot called. "Bex, is that you?" He heard the sound of the door unlocking.

The door opened about half an inch, and an eye peered through the door at Elliot before slamming quickly.

"Bex?" Elliot called out again. "Bex, it's me, Elliot!" he said, pleading with Rebecca.

After a few quiet moments, the door opened again. Elliot pushed the door open lightly and found Rebecca sitting on the floor a few feet away.

Rebecca was looking at him with watery eyes. Teary trails ran down her cheeks.

Elliot entered the apartment and closed the door behind him. He crouched down onto the floor near Rebecca but still far enough away to give her some distance. "Hey, Bex," he said.

"How?" she whispered. "How are you alive?" she asked, sounding somewhat upset.

"I'm here now. I'm alive," Elliot said, moving in closer.

Rebecca pushed him. "We had a funeral for you!" she said, her eyes filling with tears. "I thought you were dead. For three whole years! Where the hell have you been?" Rebecca started to cry.

Elliot moved in and wrapped his arms around Rebecca, giving her a hug. "It's a long story."

"You smell like a fish market," said Bex, pulling her head away and wiping the tears from her face. "Go take a shower," she ordered. "Then you can tell me where you've been fucking off for the past three years," she added.

They both stood up from the floor and looked at each other.

"I had stopped by May's place before I came here an uh—"

"Yeah, I know …" said Bex. "We can talk about that later." Bex pointed to a bunch of boxes in the living room. "I, uhh, I grabbed your stuff from the apartment. All your clothes are there so you should be able to find something. I'll put some coffee on in the meantime."

Elliot wiped away the steam that had collected on the mirror. He braced his hands on the sides of the sink and looked at himself in the mirror. His hair used to be brown, but under the curse of the Reaper, it had changed to black. He looked down and shaped his hair with his hands, making it look neat. When his eyes returned to the mirror, a skeleton was looking back at him. He gasped and stepped backward, rubbing his eyes. When he looked back at the mirror, only his own reflection looked back at him.

Rebecca had made coffee and was sitting in her breakfast nook, looking out the window. "Coffee's in the pot. Got some bread if you wanna make toast."

"Thanks," replied Elliot. He walked over to the counter, poured himself a cup of black coffee, and then joined Bex at the small table in the nook. "I'm glad you still have the same place." Elliot took a small sip of his coffee and then looked out the window at the city. "Wasn't sure where else to go."

Rebecca had so many questions that picking one seemed impossible. "I guess I'll just start at the beginning," she finally said. "News came about your plane crashing over the Pacific Ocean." She pushed her red hair out of her face and took a sip of coffee. "Search crews looked for over a week. They found a few bodies but said that there was no way anyone survived the crash."

Elliot nodded his head, remembering the terrifying moments of panic-stricken passengers screaming and yelling before the plane went down. "Yeah," he choked out.

"What happened? We all thought you were dead."

Elliot blew air out of his nose as he chuckled. "Yeah, so did I." He took another sip of coffee. "Washed up on some island out in the middle of nowhere. Lived in the jungles for a little while, then I was able to gain trust with the locals and lived with them."

"For three years?" Bex asked.

Elliot nodded.

"How did you get back here?" Bex prodded.

"A freighter picked me up." Elliot remembered the mercenaries, led by a man named Novak, ransacking local villages and kidnapping people. He remembered being locked up on the freighter like an animal and being tortured for amusement.

Rebecca reached out and touched Elliot's arm. "I'm glad you're back," she said, reassuring him with a smile.

"I feel like I should be glad but—"

"May?"

"Yeah." Elliot looked down at his coffee and thought about her, lost in memory. "I held on to a picture of her the whole time," he said in a somber tone.

"She thought you were dead. *Everyone* did."

"I know." Elliot rotated his coffee cup around for no reason. "I … I don't blame her. I just … I dunno."

"Your brother will be happy to see you," said Bex, trying to change the subject from May.

"How's he doing?" Elliot asked, thankful the subject was changed.

"Still throwing lavish parties, but his dad plans on running for mayor and handing the company over to Matthew."

Matthew was Elliot's biological older brother who looked exactly like him. The boys were separated when they were kids and placed into separate foster homes. Matthew ended up being adopted by the CEO of a Fortune 500 company and his wife, who had always wanted a kid but were unable to have one of their own. To them, Matthew was a gift from God, and they treated him as such.

"Speaking of which," Bex said, before taking another sip of coffee, "you should probably go down to city hall and get your death certificate rescinded."

"Shit, yeah, you're right. I wonder how difficult that is. I'm sure it's not something they deal with every day."

"Maybe Mr. Folds could help you out? I'm sure he has connections," Bex suggested. "And while you're at it, maybe get yourself a haircut? You look like hammered shit," she said with a smirk.

"True," Elliot agreed. "But I don't want him telling Matthew I'm back before I do," he added. "I'll figure it out."

"Well, you think on it. If you want, you can come to work with me, and I'll have one of the cooks make you breakfast."

"Yeah, all right. Thanks, Bex."

Having finally gotten his death certificate rescinded after spending hours in city hall, Elliot was glad to finally leave the building. But that happiness faded quickly when he was swarmed by a group of people, all waving cameras and microphones in his face and yelling questions at him.

"Mr. Blythe! Where have you been all these years?" one man yelled.

"Elliot Blythe! What was it like surviving a plane crash?" another man asked.

"Mr. Blythe, is it true the plane was hijacked by terrorists?" one woman yelled while almost hitting Elliot in the face with a microphone.

A hand reached through the crowd of raving reporters, grabbed Elliot by his shirt, and pulled him through all the people.

"How ya doin', Tiger?" The hand that had saved Elliot from the crowd slapped him on the back of his shoulder.

It was Elliot's brother, Matthew, wearing dark sunglasses and a flashy gray suit. He gave Elliot a hug, almost squeezing the breath out of him. "So good to see ya!" he yelled, leading Elliot to a limo with an open back door and pushing him inside.

The two of them got settled inside the limo, sitting across from one another.

Matthew removed his sunglasses and tucked them into his jacket pocket. "So, little buddy," he said, pouring scotch into a couple highball glasses. "What's it like coming back from the dead?" he asked, handing Elliot his glass. Matthew sat back in his seat, resting his arms on top of the headrests, and crossed one of his legs almost as if to show off how well he had been doing.

Under normal circumstances, Elliot probably would've laughed at his comment, but in light of recent events, the humor escaped him. "How'd you know I was here?" Elliot took his first sip of alcohol in three years, and the way it burned going down his throat felt refreshing to him.

"Henry got a call from one of his staff in the hall," replied Matthew.

Elliot nodded his head and took another sip of his drink. "I wanted you to hear it from me."

"Ah, forget it. I'm just glad you're back, Tiger!" he said, raising his glass in Elliot's direction.

Elliot clinked his glass against Matthew's, and they drank.

"Was a real kick to the boys when I heard about the accident," Matthew said in a somber tone.

"Drown your sorrows in booze and strippers?" Elliot asked lightheartedly, trying to bring humor to the situation.

"Y'know they say it'll cure anything." Matthew smirked.

"Yeah, nothing a few lap dances won't fix, right?"

They both laughed.

"It really is good to have you back, little brother. Life seems to be on a mission to keep us two degenerates away from each other."

Elliot reminisced about all the trouble they had caused together before being split and put into separate foster homes. "It's good to be back."

"I'm gonna be throwin' a little bash tonight. You're the guest of honor so make sure you're there." Matthew finished his drink.

"Can't wait!" Elliot remembered he had to meet Valentine that night. "What time?" he asked Matthew.

"'Bout nine."

"Might be a little fashionably late," replied Elliot. "I have to meet someone tonight."

"Mmm, already making midnight movies?" Matthew joked.

Elliot laughed. "No, it's not like that. I'll be there though."

"Well, bring them along if you'd like—the bigger the party, the better."

Valentine didn't strike Elliot as the sociable type, and he certainly didn't want to spend any more time with him than he had to.

"Henry will want to see you, no doubt," said Matthew. He always referred to Henry by his name, never as his father.

"It'll be good to see everyone again," replied Elliot.

CHAPTER 3

OF LOVE AND DEATH

Elliot arrived at the address written on the paper that Valentine had given him at eight o'clock. "This can't be right," Elliot said to himself. He looked at the paper and then up at the number written on the farmhouse. Elliot walked up the gravel path and up to the front door. He grabbed the brass knocker and banged it a few times.

An old man opened the door and greeted Elliot. "Good evening."

"Erm, I'm sorry. I think I have the wrong address," said Elliot. "I'm looking for someone named Valentine?" He meant it as a statement, but it came out sounding more like a question.

"Ah!" the old man exclaimed in realization. "You must be Mister Blythe. Mister Valentine has been expecting you." The man stepped to the side of the doorway and waved Elliot inside. "Come in! Come in!" The old man closed the door behind him. "My name is Warren. I work here as the groundskeeper. Mister Valentine is just up ahead in the other room."

"How long have you known him?" Elliot asked.

"Oh, a good number of years. Good man, that Valentine. Saved my life more times than I can count." He was a short man, bald on the top of his head but had a stripe of gray hair that ran around the sides. Walking with a slight limp, he made his way through the interestingly decorated house.

Elliot noticed that Valentine must have a passion for history as he looked at old war flags placed in frames and mounted on the walls. Vintage swords were grasped in hook displays under the flags, perhaps from the respective countries of the flags they were under. Valentine also had a passion for art. Elliot stopped to look at an authentic Claude Monet in an ornate gold frame.

"Mister Valentine is an admirer of impressionists," said Warren.

"It's beautiful," Elliot commented.

"Quite the appetite for history as well," Warren added.

Warren led Elliot to a large room where two men were fighting each other with swords. One of the two men was trying desperately to parry his opponent's attacks with vicious clangs of steel.

The attacker wouldn't let up. Stepping into his opponent, he let loose a flurry of quick strikes and slashes, thrusting his sword inward and stepping to the side as he yanked his sword back and sent his opponent's blade across the room.

"Mister Valentine!" called Warren. "Mister Blythe has arrived."

Valentine, still holding his sword, looked in his direction. "Ah, Elliot, good!" he said, placing his sword on a rack of many others. Then he walked over to Elliot. "Made it through your first day, I see." He wasn't at all what Elliot expected. Valentine was tall and well built with jet-black hair pushed to the side with a trimmed black goatee to match. Instead of black, smoky robes, he wore a fine collared shirt and gray suit pants.

"I, uh, I can't stay too long. My brother is throwing this party for me," said Elliot.

Warren left.

"What time?" asked Valentine, sounding intrigued.

"Nine."

"Perfect! Can't wait!" replied Valentine, inviting himself. "In the meantime, we have some work to do."

"What kind of work, exactly?" asked Elliot nervously. "You're not gonna drug me again, are you?"

Valentine laughed. "No, that was a one-time thing, hopefully. Tonight, I want to teach you a few things." He led Elliot to the back of the room and opened a glass slider leading to a fancy stone patio outside. "The first thing I want to show you is how to take control of the Reaper."

"How do I do that?"

"It's quite easy actually. Watch." Valentine stepped out onto the patio under the light of the moon. "Now, the Reaper is *much* stronger at night, allowing you to take on its form and powers."

"Does it hurt?" Elliot asked, cocking his head slightly to the side.

Valentine chuckled. "No. Just watch. Just relax, and let it do its thing." Valentine tilted his head to the sky, and a thick black smoke poured down over his head and rolled down his body, covering him completely.

When the smoke had cleared, Valentine stood dressed in a long black cloak. A subtle smoke rolled from his cowl down his shoulders, clinging to his cloak and dancing freely in the breeze. A black tunic replaced his white collared shirt, and a crimson cloth was wrapped around his waist like a belt. His flesh was gone, and only a clean skull lit by the moonlight looked back at Elliot.

"Well?" asked Valentine, holding his arms out to the side.

"And I can do that too?" Elliot was still confused.

"Yes, now just relax, and let the Reaper work its magic."

Elliot was nervous and could feel his heart beating out of control. He looked up at the stars and closed his eyes. He could feel something inside him moving like it was trying to break free. Elliot took a breath and relaxed his muscles. He felt a sudden sense of relief as a cold feeling washed over his head and down his body.

Elliot looked down at fleshless hands. He turned his head and looked at his black robes, which emitted a thick smoke. His tunic was black and gray and was tied at the waist by a black belt.

"How do you feel?" asked Valentine.

Elliot was processing everything. He could feel a strong sense of freedom and relief. He was stress free and felt great. "It feels ... amazing," he said. "I feel ... free." Elliot stretched his arms. "So what now?"

"Here, hold this," replied Valentine, handing Elliot an apple.

"What am I supposed to do with this?"

"The Reaper is capable of many things, but it comes at a cost."

"Which is ... apples?"

"No," Valentine said bluntly. "The apple is just a symbol. The Reaper relies on the consumption of life in order to maintain existence."

"So what exactly does that entail?" Elliot wasn't quite sure he liked where this was going.

"You have to take a life to save yours."

"To save *my* life?"

"Without the consumption of human life, the Reaper will completely take over what's left of your existence, and it will consume you. Your mind would be destroyed by the darkness, and you would be no more than a mere puppet to the Reaper."

Elliot could tell by Valentine's tone that he wasn't messing around. "I don't want people to suffer, and I don't want to hurt anyone."

"You're looking at this in a 'the glass is completely empty' sort of way. Death isn't all about dying; it's about giving life." Valentine was hoping to get a broader message across.

"How do you mean?" Elliot was confused.

"Death provides life for all sorts of things. Look over here." Valentine led Elliot to a large garden patch. "Every spring, I dig everything up and fill it in with fresh compost that I make. The nutrients of the compost are all made up of once living things, thus not only providing life for my vegetables but a *better* life."

"Y'know, I never pictured you as a gardener when I first met you."

"Hey, everyone's gotta have a hobby. Anyway, are you following me so far?" Valentine asked.

"Yeah, I think so."

"Now think of the vegetables like people, and the compost is dead people."

"*What?*" Elliot was completely confused now. "You've lost me."

"Yeah ... probably ... probably not the best way to phrase that." Valentine rubbed his chin. "All right, let's try this again," he started. "I know it's probably been a while since you've watched the news. Not that any of it is really worth watching though. It's all the same old bullshit and rhetoric."

"Okay ...?"

"The world is filled with horrible people, Elliot. I'm sure you can attest to that, yes?"

Elliot remembered being on the island and witnessing the mercenaries sacking villages, kidnapping people from their homes, and even raping some of the women. He nodded his head. "Yeah," he said.

"Some people aren't really people; they're *animals*." Valentine's tone started to fill with anger, but he didn't raise his voice. "Sick fucks in this world who commit heinous crimes and get away with it. *Animals* who prey on children. Drunks who go home and take out their insecurities on their family. Rapists, murderers, thugs, sadists, pedophiles. By taking out people like that, not only could you provide life but a *better* life for people. One less rapist or pedophile in the world could change an untold number of lives." Valentine spoke with such passion and vigor.

Elliot nodded his head. He was starting to understand. "Is that what you do?" he asked.

Valentine nodded. "I grew up here in Sterling, and I've devoted my life to looking after its people. I have an amazing power, and so do you." He looked at Elliot. "I like knowing I can make a difference in this world, but it's a hard job for just one person."

Valentine's words got to Elliot. He felt empowered and motivated. He nodded his head; he wanted to make a difference. "So what do I do with this apple?" he asked Valentine.

"Hold it in your hand out in front of you."

Elliot extended his arm, holding the apple in his bony palm.

"Focus, feel the life within the apple. Though the Reaper draws its main source of power from the souls it collects, you can draw extra boosts of energy from the things around you. But it'll come at a cost." Valentine nodded toward the apple.

Elliot focused. He looked at the apple and controlled his breath. A small black pool of smoke swirled around the bottom of the apple. "I can feel it!"

"Good, keep focusing. Reach into the apple, and drain its energy."

Elliot focused harder on the apple. The black smoke wrapped higher around the apple as it started to turn brown and rot.

The apple was reduced to a withered brown core, and the smoke in Elliot's hand dissipated.

"Holy shit!" Elliot exclaimed.

"Nice. You're doing well," Valentine complimented. "The Reaper can draw a limited amount of raw energy from the living things around you."

"So, like …" Elliot was still trying to process everything that was going on and was having a hard time finding his thoughts. "Can we die?" he finally asked.

"I mean, for the most part, no, not really."

"For the most part?" Elliot asked, feeling like Valentine wasn't telling him everything.

"Well, Reapers can kill each other."

"So, there are others, like us?"

"Yes. But I wouldn't go looking for any of them. Most aren't as forgiving as I am."

"How does a Reaper kill another Reaper?"

"Do you plan on killing me?" Valentine asked sarcastically.

"Just for, y'know, *insurance* purposes."

"Follow me," said Valentine, leading Elliot back inside the house.

As they entered the house, a black smoke swirled around each of them, and the persona of the Reaper faded, leaving Valentine and Elliot in their human flesh.

"Take these," said Valentine. He took two short swords with curved steel blades and handed them to Elliot. "These were my first swords. Take care of them."

Elliot marveled at the swords. The pitch-black sheen of the blades contrasted with the cloth-covered crimson hilts.

"They're scythe blades," Valentine said. "Eventually, we'll get you better swords, ones forged from the souls of the damned in a place called the Outer Darkness. Only a sword forged with damned souls can kill a Reaper."

"Thanks, Valentine. I'll take care of them." Elliot tucked the swords under his arm.

"Give your swords to the Reaper. It'll hold them for you," said Valentine.

A black smoke wrapped around Elliot's swords before they vanished.

"What is the Outer Darkness?" Elliot asked.

"I'll show you some time, fun place. In the meantime, how are you with a sword?" Valentine asked.

"I was taught to use one by a tribe of warriors back when I was on the island," Elliot replied.

"Excellent. Prepare to further your training." Valentine handed Elliot a longer, two-handed sword as he drew his own from the rack. He raised the sword vertically and then pointed it at Elliot.

"Wait … What are we doing?" Elliot asked. A look of shock lit up his eyes as Valentine lunged at him.

Valentine swung his sword horizontally, but Elliot jumped backward.

The blade connected with a lamp and shattered it. He swung his sword at Elliot again, this time meeting Elliot's blade in the air.

Elliot pushed Valentine off to give himself some space.

Valentine jumped onto the coffee table and leaped at Elliot.

Elliot dropped and rolled to his right, swinging his sword at Valentine but missing him by mere inches. He kicked a footrest into the air at Valentine, but he chopped it in half with one swing.

Valentine swung his blade downward at Elliot.

Elliot dodged the blade with another roll, causing it to lodge itself in the wooden floor. Elliot jumped to his feet and swung downward at Valentine, who ripped his sword from the floor and parried the attack, stepping to Elliot's left and grazing his ribs with the tip of his sword. Elliot winced from the pain and put his hand to the wound. "There's no blood," he said.

"Reapers don't bleed," replied Valentine, before making another aggressive strike at Elliot.

Stepping to the side as Valentine's blade ran down the length of his own, Elliot used his right hand to punch Valentine in the face.

"Clever," Valentine commended. He raised his hand and shot a shadowy mass at Elliot, sending him backward. He advanced on Elliot and swung his sword downward.

Elliot blocked Valentine's swing and kicked his feet out from under him, causing him to fall. Elliot rolled to his feet and pointed his sword at Valentine before he could get up.

"Excellent work," said Valentine. "Perhaps I underestimated you," he added.

"Is that what you're telling yourself?" Elliot asked.

Valentine flashed a grin. He shot another burst of dark energy at Elliot, knocking him up into the air. He sprang to his feet, grabbed Elliot with the force of the Reaper, pinned him to the ground, and extended his sword toward Elliot's face. "Fold," he demanded.

Elliot released his grip on his swords and showed Valentine his palms.

Valentine smiled widely. "We gotta get you to that shindig. Great opportunity to people watch," he said, looking at the clock.

"Shindig?" asked Elliot. "Who the fuck says that?"

"*I* do," insisted Valentine.

"How do you shoot the bursts of energy like that?"

"Think of the Reaper as an extension of yourself. Bend the Reaper's powers to your will, and it will do your bidding. The Reaper is capable of many great things, as well as many *horrible* things."

"Hey, Tiger!" said Matthew as he greeted Elliot with a drink in his hand.

"Matthew," he said, extending his other hand to Valentine.

"Valentine," he replied, greeting Matthew's hand with a shake.

The three of them entered the Folds' estate for the party that Matthew had put together. The mansion was packed with people, some of whom Elliot recognized, but most were complete strangers. Everyone was dressed in fine suits and dresses. Some people danced, while others drank and talked among themselves.

"You're a friend of Elliot's?" Matthew asked Valentine.

"He's actually the one who found me and brought me back here," Elliot butted in.

"Yeah," said Valentine, going along with the story. "Found the poor sap clinging to a raft of coconuts," he added.

"Well, hey, I'm glad you both made it. Lemme grab you guys some drinks, and we'll do a toast," Matthew said, wandering off into the crowd of people.

"Coconuts?" Elliot asked.

"Hey, this was an impromptu thing; we never rehearsed a story."

Matthew came back with drinks and handed them to Elliot and Valentine. He took a fork and clinked it against his glass, gathering everyone's attention. "Hello, everyone," he started off. "I'd like to thank all of you for being here. It's a very special occasion, because my brother, who we all thought was dead, has come back to the land of the living. So let's raise a glass to Elliot." Matthew raised his glass in Elliot's direction.

Valentine raised his glass, and so did everyone else, followed by a brief cheer before everyone went back to what they were doing.

"It's so good to have you back, my boy. You have been sorely missed," said Henry Folds, a tall, silver-haired man with a sharp chin. He embraced

Elliot, overwhelming him with the scents of old cologne and stale cigar smoke.

"Can I steal you for a minute?" Matthew asked Elliot.

"Yeah, lead the way," he said to Matthew. "You gonna be okay on your own, or do I need to get you a babysitter?" he asked Valentine.

"Well, if you know any cute redheads, you can send them my way. I'll be at the bar." Valentine gave a sheepish grin before wandering away and introducing himself to a woman at the bar.

Matthew led Elliot down a hallway.

"What's up?" Elliot asked.

"Well, as you've probably heard, Henry is gonna be running for office, and I'm gonna be taking his seat in the holding firm. Was wondering if you might need a job."

"Hell of an offer," replied Elliot.

"Yeah, think on it, y'know?" Matthew led Elliot into the library and poured two glasses of scotch. "Really am glad to have you back, Elliot." Matthew handed him a glass. "You're the only *real* family I have."

Meanwhile, Valentine was sitting at the bar, his eyes scanning the crowd of people around him. He spotted a man who appeared to be making a girl uncomfortable. The man kept leaning into her and touching her, and then he walked over to the bar next to Valentine.

"How's it going?" Valentine asked the man. "Here with your wife?"

"Two martinis, dry," the man said to the bartender. "Nah," he replied to Valentine. "Just trying to find a little something to take home for the night," he said, taking the drinks from the bartender.

Valentine saw the man slip something into one of the drinks.

The man returned to the table and set the drinks on it.

"How's it goin'?" asked Elliot.

"Well," replied Valentine, taking a sip of his scotch. "Watch this." Valentine gestured to the man who was continuing to make the young woman uncomfortable. Valentine made a small twisting motion with his hand, and the drinks the man set down slowly moved and changed places.

The man, oblivious to the moving drinks, picked his up and insisted the woman drink as well. They each took a sip, and within a minute, the man began to stagger before he slumped to the ground and fell unconscious.

"What the hell was that?" Elliot asked Valentine.

"Guy roofied her drink. I just switched them. Stupid fuck roofied himself."

"So what do we do now?" asked Elliot.

"I'll take care of it. You just stay here." Valentine walked over to the unconscious man. "Looks like someone had a little too much to drink," he said to the woman. Valentine picked up the man, hoisted him onto his shoulder, and then took him out of sight.

"Met the owner of this fine estate while you were away," said Valentine when he returned.

"Mister Folds? That's my brother's adoptive father, good man. Whatchya think of him?" Elliot asked.

"Not too bad of a guy, I suppose," said Valentine, despite thinking that Folds was just another crooked politician.

Just then, something caught Elliot's attention.

It was May, slowly making her way through the crowd of people. Her head swiveled as she scanned the room, her bright-blue eyes looking for a familiar face.

Elliot turned to hide his face from sight, but it was too late; May had seen him.

"Uh, hi, Elliot," she said nervously.

Elliot acted as if he hadn't seen her approach. "Oh, hey, May." May was the last person he wanted to see.

"Saw on the news that you were alive and back in the city." May nervously twirled a finger in her hair.

"Yep, here I am," Elliot replied.

"I kinda thought I'd hear news like that from you and not a news reporter," said May.

"Well, this has been a gas, but I'm gonna split and leave you two alone," said Valentine, excusing himself from his seat.

"Uh, nah, you can stay," insisted Elliot. He gave Valentine a look that said, "Don't leave me here."

"I couldn't. I don't want to intrude." Valentine smirked at Elliot as if to say he knew what was going on. "Might go play a little bingo in the back."

Bingo? Elliot thought to himself.

"So ... how have you been?" asked May.

"Do you really care?" asked Elliot, an offensive tone in his voice. "Does your boyfriend know you're here?"

May scoffed. "I thought you were dead, Elliot," she replied. "For *three* years, I might add. You act like I didn't wait for you, but I *did*. And eventually, I had to move on with my life."

Elliot shook his head and then pulled a drink closer to him. "You were the only thing keeping me going," he finally said.

"I'm sorry, Elliot," said May. She tried to put a hand on Elliot's shoulder, but he leaned away from it. "Even after all this time, you still haven't changed," she accused.

"Just leave," said Elliot.

Elliot frantically went looking for Valentine, and to his surprise, he found him dancing with his sister, Rebecca. Elliot grabbed Valentine by the shoulder. "Hey, we need to go."

Valentine turned, his hands still on Rebecca's waist and his head resting on hers. "So soon?" he asked.

"Yes, now." Elliot pulled Valentine's arm, ripping him from the dance.

Elliot and Valentine walked out of a cloud of darkness and onto a small mountain that overlooked the city. The light of the moon turned them both into their Reaper forms.

Elliot sat down on the rocky ledge and looked at the city lights glowing in the night.

"Listen, if this was about that dance with your sister ..." said Valentine sitting next to Elliot.

"It's not," replied Elliot.

"What's got you so hot and bothered then?" Valentine asked.

"That girl you left me alone with was my ex."

"Ah, yeah, I could sense some tension between you two. Leave off on a bad note?"

Elliot shook his head. "She left because she thought I was fucking *dead* for three fucking years," he said angrily.

Valentine pulled a joint of Malice from his robes and lit it between his fingers. The light of the cherry glowed a bright orange on his skull. He exhaled the smoke. "I know it's a shitty situation," he said. "But you shouldn't be mad at her."

"I'm not mad at her. I'm mad at *myself*," Elliot buried his skull in his bony hands.

Valentine took another drag. He wasn't quite sure what Elliot wanted to hear. "Went through a similar experience once," he finally said.

Elliot didn't say anything, but he turned his head to imply he was listening and for Valentine to continue.

"Her name was Gwendolyn Lace," said Valentine, taking another drag. "Gwen," he said quietly to himself. He offered Elliot the joint.

Elliot accepted it and took a drag. "So, what happened?" he asked.

"Weren't together for very long, only a few months. But damn did I love her." Valentine let out a heavy sigh. "Her heart eventually started to weaken. I stayed by her hospital bed day and night. Things started taking a turn for the worse."

"What did you do?" asked Elliot, taking another drag before handing it back to Valentine.

"One night, a woman with black wings came into her room and bargained my life for Gwen's."

"And that's how you became a Reaper," said Elliot.

Valentine nodded. "I took the deal, and Gwen quickly recovered. But after that, she said I wasn't the same person anymore. In her words, I was 'cold, calloused, and jaded.' So she left me for someone else." Valentine took a long drag and held it in.

"Well, I mean, you were a Reaper. Couldn't you have just killed the guy?" Elliot asked.

Valentine nodded. "I thought about it."

"Why didn't you?"

"Because he made her happy." Valentine looked down. "Something I could never do," he said in a choked voice. He let out a shaky sigh.

Elliot wasn't quite sure what to say. Valentine's words hit him deep in the center of his chest. "I want May to be happy. I just … wish she was happy with *me*."

Valentine handed the joint back to Elliot.

Elliot took a drag. "What do I do?" he asked.

"Wish her the best … and hope the same for yourself."

Elliot wanted to do that, but he just couldn't accept it. On one hand, he wanted to forget all about her. But on the other hand, he didn't.

"Much like yourself, I was mad at her at first. But I got over that." Valentine took the joint back and took a drag. "I just … never got over the love." He took another drag and then crushed the cherry in the dirt. "The way I see it, every person is like a book. Each day is a new page, and the best we can do is live our stories one page at a time. Your story is still being written, so turn the pages slowly, and enjoy it. If you're lucky, one day, your stories will come together again."

Elliot nodded, somewhat lost in thought. "Maybe."

"No, I mean it, someone is literally writing your story right now, probably using their computer or something. In fact, the writer is probably using this as a buffer because they're not sure what's going to happen next."

Elliot raised his brow and gave Valentine a bewildered look.

"Anyway," said Valentine. "You've got a good family; they all really care about you."

"Yeah, my brother Matthew, and you met Bex already."

"Matthew seems like a pretty cool cat. Parents?" asked Valentine.

Elliot shook his head no. "You? Got any family?" he asked.

"Sadly, no," replied Valentine.

The next morning, Elliot awoke to the sound of someone knocking on Rebecca's apartment door. Rebecca had left earlier in the morning for work so that left Elliot to answer the door. He rolled off the couch and stood up, draping the blanket around his shoulders. He answered the door.

Two police officers stood in the hallway outside Rebecca's apartment.

"Are you Elliot Blythe?" asked the officer to Elliot's left.

"Might be. Why?" asked Elliot, still half asleep.

The two officers exchanged glances.

"I'm sorry to be the one to tell you this, but your brother Matthew was murdered. He has you listed as his next of kin."

Elliot felt as though his heart stopped and his blood rushed to his head, making him dizzy. The words made him sick to his stomach, but it felt like there was a knot in his throat. He felt as though he had just been hit by a cheap blow to the gut. At a loss for words, he nodded silently to the officers and closed the door. He walked into the kitchen and grabbed a bottle of rum from the cupboard. He put a glass down on the counter and paused for a moment while looking at the glass. He raised the bottle to his lips and downed half of it.

Elliot sat down on the floor and leaned against the counter. He buried his head in his knees and grieved for his brother.

Elliot grabbed his phone and called Valentine. "I need a favor."

That evening, Elliot's phone rang.

"Hello?" Elliot asked.

"Elliot?" the caller asked.

"Yeah? Who's this?"

"Erm, sorry, it's Henry, Matthew's father."

"Ah, hi, Mister Folds. How are you holding up?" Elliot asked.

"I'm managing. It's hard losing a child, even if they aren't truly yours. I'm sorry for your loss, son. Matthew really loved you. How are you doing?"

"I just wish I had gotten more time with him."

"I know, son. But he was overjoyed to have you back," Mr. Folds replied. "I hope you're staying safe. If you need a place, my doors are open," he said, changing the topic.

"I appreciate the offer, but I'll be all right. I'm staying with my sister for the moment."

"Good, good. Well, just remember, I'm here if you need anything."

Elliot greatly appreciated the offer. "Same here, sir."

CHAPTER 4

THE CHEMIST

Elliot and Valentine sat perched on a rooftop overlooking one of the Sterling City Police precincts. They were both cloaked in darkness, their skulls illuminated by the moonlight.

Valentine took one last drag of malice before he crushed the joint on the rooftop. "Police radio chatter says they picked up a potential suspect in your brother's murder," he said.

"Got a way in?" Elliot asked. He was determined to find the person responsible for his brother's murder at all costs.

"Police commissioner owes me a few favors," Valentine replied. "Unfortunately, I don't think this will count as one of them."

"So what's the plan?"

"I'll cut the power to the building and create a distraction. That'll give you an opportunity to sneak into the cell block and find your guy. Here, put this in your hood; it'll allow us to keep in touch." Valentine handed Elliot an earpiece.

"Any idea who I'm looking for?" asked Elliot.

"Don't have a name, but I would start at the interrogation room and make my way from there. You won't have too much time, so make it quick, got it?"

"Got it," Elliot assured him.

"Stay here. I'll tell you when." Valentine vanished into the darkness.

Valentine cut the power to the precinct, and the building went dark. He turned to a nearby truck. With a wave of his hand, the brakes released, and the truck rolled into a storefront across the street from the precinct.

The distraction worked as Valentine had hoped. Police officers soon filled the street to investigate the situation and restore power.

"Now's your chance. Get in there," Valentine said into his transceiver.

Elliot traveled through the darkness and entered the police precinct. "I'm in," he said to Valentine.

"Good. Overheard some of the officers. Your guy is in the interrogation room," replied Valentine.

"On my way now." Elliot found the interrogation room. He passed through the locked door as if they weren't there at all. As he entered the room, the lights flickered.

The man handcuffed to the table was startled at the ghostly sight and tried yanking himself free from the restraint.

"Breaking out of those cuffs won't help you," said Elliot. He waved his hands, and the cuffs released. Before the man could react, Elliot extended his hand and shot a bolt of darkness that struck the man and threw him across the room. Elliot extended his hand again, and grabbing the man with an invisible force, he lifted him and slammed him against the floor.

The man spit blood onto the floor. "What are you? What do you want?" he choked out.

"You killed a man," replied Elliot.

The man chuckled and wiped the blood from his mouth. "I have killed many men."

"Matthew Blythe," said Elliot.

"Ah, the rich pig," the man replied.

Elliot stepped forward and kicked the man in the chest. "Who hired you?" he demanded.

"I don't answer to ghosts." The man scoffed, clutching his ribs.

"You will." Elliot removed his swords, and with one quick motion, he severed both the man's arms and sheathed his swords.

The man howled at the agonizing pain, blood pouring from his severed extremities.

Elliot lifted the man into the air using the Reaper's power. "Who hired you?" he demanded again. Closing his fist caused the man to start choking.

"He wasn't ... the target," the man gasped.

The lights in the building came back on, and Valentine's voice came through the earpiece. "Time's up, kid; they're coming your way."

"Who *was*?" Elliot asked the man, tightening his fist.

The man choked for air. His skin started to wither and wrinkle, and his eyes started sinking into his skull. Elliot was draining the life from the man. "His ... brother ..."

Elliot was shocked at the man's answer. He opened his fist, and the man's lifeless body crumpled to the floor.

"Get the fuck out of there, kid!" came Valentine's voice from the earpiece.

Elliot could hear officers starting to unlock the door.

"What did you find out?" asked Valentine.

"My brother wasn't the target." Elliot watched the commotion below him as emergency medical services arrived at the precinct.

"So, who was?"

"I am," replied Elliot.

"So they mistook your brother for you," Valentine pointed out.

"Seems that way."

"You sure make enemies pretty quick. Any idea who's behind it?"

Elliot shook his head no. "I have a feeling though."

"Got a way of figuring that out?" Valentine asked.

"I think so," Elliot replied. "But I'm gonna need your help."

"No problem. I've got something I have to do right now, but I'll meet up with you later, and we can discuss the next step."

Valentine sneaked into the home of Sam Dorset, also known as "the Hammer." He was the leader of one of the many gangs in Sterling City. Dorset was best known for bludgeoning his victims to death with a clawhammer, and Valentine had decided something should be done about his reign of violence.

Valentine watched from the shadows and dark crevices of the home as Dorset went through his nightly routine.

Dorset turned the lights off, giving Valentine full range of the house without being detected.

As Dorset lay in bed, he was overcome with the strange sensation of someone standing in the room with him. He sat up in bed and looked around the room. Seeing nothing, he put his head back on his pillow.

Valentine moved silently through the darkness, closer to Dorset. He extended a bony hand out of the shadows, grabbed Dorset by the throat, and yanked him into the darkness.

Police Commissioner Lowell paced around the vacant rooftop of an apartment building not too far from the precinct.

Valentine emerged out of nowhere from the darkness. "Good, you made it."

"You broke into my precinct and killed my murder suspect. Of course I was going to be here!" barked the commissioner.

"I had a personal interest in your man that took precedence," Valentine replied calmly.

"You had no right!" the commissioner insisted. "We had a deal: you do your thing, and you leave the police alone."

"I have altered the deal," Valentine said firmly.

"You're no better than the thugs we pull off the streets. You're just a self-righteous murderer."

"If my methods displease you, then perhaps it's time I replace you with someone more … open-minded." Valentine raised his tone slightly. "You and your men don't do anything for this city."

"You don't think we could take care of this city without you?" Lowell huffed.

"I don't think you could boil water." Valentine crossed his arms. "I brought you a gift, but now I'm thinking I should keep it for myself."

The commissioner gave Valentine a look of confusion.

Valentine created a pool of black smoke in the air. Reaching into it, he pulled out Dorset from the darkness.

"Holy fuck." The commissioner was shocked at the sight of the gang leader before him. "How the fuck did you get him?" he asked.

"My own methods," Valentine replied. "If you can come to respect that, perhaps we could help each other. The law has … restrictions, whereas I do not."

The commissioner nodded. "So what now?"

"I trust you'll see to it that he never walks free again."

"And the suspect you murdered?" asked Lowell.

"Dorset is your new suspect."

"The victim died from a gunshot wound," said Lowell.

"Perhaps he defended himself, and Dorset was unable to use his traditional methods," said Valentine, turning to leave.

"Wait! One more thing," Lowell called.

"What is it?" asked Valentine.

"We found a body at the beach and then two dead at the morgue. You know anything about that?"

"I'm afraid not, Commissioner," Valentine replied.

Elliot was relaxing on the couch reading a book at Rebecca's apartment. An unexpected knock came from the door. Elliot put his book on the coffee table and got up to see who it was. He wasn't expecting anyone, and Rebecca wouldn't be home for another hour.

Elliot peered through the eye hole in the door and saw six men standing in the hallway, armed with either a pistol or a rifle.

Before Elliot could make a break from the door, the lead man fired three shots through the door, one of which ripped through Elliot's hip.

Collapsing to the floor in agony, he crawled to the coffee table, grabbed his phone, and quickly called Valentine. "I'm at Bex's apartment. There's a bunch of guys here, and one of them shot me." Elliot was waiting to hear a reply from Valentine when all of a sudden the men in the hallway began screaming, yelling, and frantically firing their weapons.

Valentine was on the roof of a high-rise overlooking the city when he got the call from Elliot. He immediately sprang into action without saying a word to Elliot. He jumped into a portal of darkness.

Valentine saw the men in the hallway. As he emerged from the darkness, all the lights in the hall went out except for one that flickered over Valentine's head.

The men turned to face the ghostly apparition at the end of the hall and raised their weapons.

Valentine reached into the darkness. Long black tentacles shot out from the shadows of the wall and grabbed three of the men.

The men screamed in horror and fired their weapons at the shadows, but each of them was ripped into the darkness and vanished.

Valentine drew his sword and rushed down the hallway like a fierce wind. With one violent horizontal swing, he cut two of the men in half at the waist. Before their torsos could hit the ground, Valentine swung his sword again and decapitated both of them.

The last man fired three shots into Valentine's chest, but all of them passed clean through as if Valentine were made completely of smoke and struck the far wall. The man rushed toward Valentine.

Sidestepping, Valentine swung his sword lazily at the man's legs, slicing the back of his knees and causing him to drop to the ground, screaming in agony.

Valentine moved in front to face the man.

The man shivered with fear at the sight of Valentine's bare skull. He tried to raise his pistol but felt paralyzed.

Valentine used his power of fear to control the man. He made a finger gun with his left hand and mirrored the man. Valentine raised his finger to his head.

Under the control of Valentine, the man put the gun to his temple.

"Do you feel dead?" asked Valentine. He curled his finger inward, causing the man to shoot himself.

Valentine swept all of the bodies into the darkness. Abandoning his Reaper form, he turned back to his normal state and knocked on the door. "Elliot! It's me!" he called out.

The locks clicked, and the door opened.

Elliot was still clutching his hip.

"What the hell was that?" Valentine asked.

"I think it was those same guys that killed my brother," replied Elliot. He removed his hand from his hip. "No blood," he whispered to himself.

"Mmm, another benefit of the Reaper, remember? Focus, and you can heal yourself."

Elliot concentrated hard on the hole in his hip. The bullet pushed through his flesh and dropped to the floor as his skin closed around the hole. "No shit."

"So seriously, what the hell is going on?"

"Must've pissed off the wrong people."

"Well, you reap what you sow," said Valentine.

Elliot closed his eyes and put his hand on his face. "This isn't the time for one of your lame puns."

Valentine blew air through his nose. "So what's the plan here?"

"Well, it's not exactly safe here right now. Can Bex and I stay at your place?"

"Yeah, that's not an issue. But what about these guys trying to hunt you?"

"I think it's time I verify a few hunches."

"So what exactly do you hope to find at a coast guard base?" Valentine asked Elliot.

"I'm *hoping* they'll have some information on that ship exploding and whether or not anyone survived."

"All right, but I have one rule before we go in there. Kill *no one.* Got it?"

"Yeah."

Elliot and Valentine kept to the shadows, sneaking their way through the military complex. As they made their way to the center of the base, they saw a group of buildings.

Groups of armed security patrolled the area.

"That one there with the antenna is probably the building you want," remarked Valentine.

"All right, let's find our way inside."

Guards patrolled the interior of the data building but were completely unaware of Elliot and Valentine.

"Server room is up ahead," said Elliot in a hushed voice.

The two made their way to a computer in the center of the room.

"I'll get you in, and then you can look for whatever it is you're looking for." Valentine concentrated his power and scrambled the programming of the computer system. He tapped a few keys and pulled up a data screen. "Your turn," he said to Elliot.

Elliot sat down at the computer and began scanning the entries in the data log. "Here it is!" Elliot exclaimed. "Six days ago, they discovered wreckage of an oil vessel."

"They find anything?" Valentine asked.

"Looks like just wreckage. Air and sea crews didn't recover any bodies."

"Not much help there," remarked Valentine.

"No, but the day before that, they have a record of a helicopter coming from sea and entering the airspace. Any local airports nearby?"

"Yeah, there's a small private one not too far from here. Think your helo is there?"

"Only one way to find out," replied Elliot.

Elliot and Valentine crept into the control tower of the private airport. Two men sat at computers with their backs turned to the duo.

Valentine extended his hand, and after a few seconds, the two men slumped forward in their seats.

"What was that?" Elliot asked.

"Just knocked them out. I'll wake them up before we leave," replied Valentine.

Elliot made his way to one of the computers. After a few moments of punching keys, he called out to Valentine, "You were right. It came through here."

"Name?"

"Mmm, hang on. Fuck …"

"What? No Name?"

"Novak," replied Elliot.

"What's that?" Valentine asked.

"*Who.* He's the guy who's been trying to kill me."

"Well, *who* is he?" Valentine asked for more clarification.

"He's a mercenary. He's the guy who kidnapped me and put me on that ship. But how does he know I survived?" Elliot propped his elbows on the table and held his face in his hands. He let out a heavy sigh. "If Novak survived, then the chemist must've survived too," Elliot said to himself.

"Who's that?" asked Valentine.

"Some crazy fuck who thought he could create his own virus."

"Did he do it?"

"He got close," Elliot replied. "But if he survived, then it's only a matter of time before he succeeds."

A couple of days earlier …

A black-haired man was staring at liquids bubbling in beakers. Vials smoked and sizzled, and a computer was spitting out numbers and percentages. A news program on the TV drew his attention away from the experiments.

"Today, Sterling City welcomes back one of its lost citizens," the anchorwoman said. "Elliot Blythe disappeared three years ago and was presumed dead when the plane he was on crashed in the Pacific Ocean."

The man stared at the television with a hard-to-read look on his face. He moved across the room and grabbed a phone from the wall.

"Hello?" said the voice on the other line.

The black-haired man spoke with a thick German accent. "It appears I require your services once more."

CHAPTER 5

THE INVESTIGATION

"Dear Lord, our father in heaven, let your presence surround us as we gather here to mourn the loss of Matthew Blythe. May you bring peace and healing to our hearts. We ask that you accept Matthew into your graceful and loving arms and protect him as you embrace him in your everlasting glory. I ask that you cover Matthew's family with your wings and guide them through these dark times. Though Matthew is gone in physical form, his spirit will continue to live on in all of us, and we find comfort knowing that he is with you in your Holy Kingdom. We thank you for the time we had with Matthew, and may fond memories of his life embrace us. Amen."

"Amen," the funeral crowd said in unison.

Elliot stood next to Matthew's casket as it was lowered into the grave. Sadness flooded his emotions, and a tear rolled from the corner of his eye. As the casket made resting contact with the dirt, his sadness was replaced by anger. He wanted to find the people responsible for his brother's death and make them suffer for what they had done. He felt robbed of his time with his brother, and now he was gone.

Valentine approached the grave with Bex clinging to one of his arms and shared his umbrella with Elliot, sheltering the three of them from the cold drizzle. He produced a flask from his pocket and took a long swig before handing it to Elliot. "We'll find the people responsible," he said, trying to comfort Elliot.

"Where are we going?" Elliot asked Valentine.

"You'll see," he replied. Valentine moved his hands in a circular motion and manifested a large mass of black smoke that molded itself into the shape of an elevator.

The elevator dinged, and the doors opened.

"The fuck is that?" Elliot asked in bewilderment.

"Please hold all questions until the end of the tour. Keep your arms and legs away from the elevator doors at all times," said Valentine, stepping onto the elevator.

Still unsure of what was going on, Elliot followed Valentine.

The elevator dinged, and the doors closed.

Elliot noticed the elevator didn't have any buttons or an emergency stop.

"Next stop, the Outer Darkness. Thank you for riding the Reaper Elevator," said Valentine, still pretending to be a tour guide.

The elevator descended further and further into darkness. As the darkness consumed the two of them, they manifested into their Reaper forms. Because they were protected by the Reaper, they were oblivious to the rapidly increasing temperature.

The elevator dinged, and the doors opened to a world of black volcanic rock illuminated by a crimson sky. Blazing infernos could be seen off in the distance.

"Follow me," said Valentine.

"Where are we?" asked Elliot. He looked at the vast expanse of where he was. He could see a menacing black castle in the distance that looked like it stretched into the red sky. Winged creatures flew overhead, some carrying various objects and some not. Gargoyle-looking creatures moved in and out of buildings carved out of the volcanic rock.

"The Outer Darkness!" Valentine exclaimed.

"And what exactly *is* this place?" Elliot asked, unsatisfied with Valentine's answer.

"It's a place for the souls of the damned, people who led horrible lives come here. It's also where us Reapers come from. Oh, and there's demons and some other shit here too. Great bar up ahead though," Valentine explained.

"So … hell?"

"No. Hell is just some place made up by Christians," Valentine said bluntly. "This is much more than that. It's a whole thriving world down here." Valentine led Elliot to a bar that was carved into the rock.

The lighting inside was blood red, and cracks of lava could be seen in the rock walls. A group of people in a zombie-like state sat around a table, playing some sort of card game with a lively woman with bright-blue hair.

"What are they playing?" asked Elliot.

"They're trying to gamble away their sins."

"Valentine!" came a booming voice from behind the bar.

"Dante!" Valentine called back and waved one of his many arms.

Dante was a strange-looking creature with pale-gray skin and long, pointed yellow teeth that protruded from his mouth. He had red, lizard-like eyes and horns on his head. Pointy gray ears penetrated his fiery red mane. His body was like that of a snake but had legs like a spider's. "How ya' been, rattle bones?" he asked Valentine.

"Oh, y'know, same old Reaper shenanigans." Valentine shook Dante's clawed hand.

"You send a lot of customers my way. How about a drink on the house?" Dante offered.

"He'll have a shot of absinthe and a methanol old fashioned," said Valentine, pointing to Elliot. "And I'll take an absinthe and a mai-tai-toxin." Valentine took his seat at the bar.

Elliot sat down beside him.

"Cheers," said Valentine, raising his glass of absinthe.

They clinked glasses and downed their shots.

Elliot tapped the bar, and Dante filled his glass. He downed the second shot and tapped for a third.

Dante filled Elliot's glass and then pushed the bottle toward him. "I'll leave this here for ya."

Elliot downed his third shot and then raised the bottle to his lips and took a few large gulps.

"You okay there, killer?" Valentine asked.

"I'm fucking *pissed*!" said Elliot, throwing his glass against the rock wall. "I hardly got to know my brother." He buried his skull in his bony hands. "I feel like we were robbed of our time together."

"What do you mean?" asked Valentine. "Didn't you grow up together?"

Elliot shook his head. "No. Our parents died when we were young, and we were split up and put into different foster homes. Didn't see him again until I was eighteen, but at that point, I was in college. And then I was fucking *dead* for three years, and within a week of me getting back, someone kills him. It's fucking bullshit!" He slammed his fist on the bar.

Valentine stared into his drink, trying to find the right words. "It may not mean much to you, but you're the closest thing to a brother I've ever had."

"You don't have any family?"

Valentine shook his head. "My parents died a long time ago. Grew up in an orphanage."

"But there haven't been any orphanages in Sterling City in like eighty years."

"Yep." Valentine downed a second shot of absinthe.

"So, how old *are* you?"

"One hundred and four."

"Jesus Christ, this whole time I thought you were the same age as me. So, that means Warren—"

"Him and I met in nineteen forty-two," Valentine said.

"So you fought in the Second World War?"

"Sure did."

"That's amazing!"

"Well, don't know if 'amazing' is the word I'd use." Valentine took a sip of his other drink. "So, what's the game plan for finding our chemist and mercenary?" asked Valentine, changing the topic.

"They could be anywhere honestly."

"Well, he must have a record of some sort. Plenty of labs around here that he could've worked at."

"Yeah, but I doubt he'll be at any of those labs."

"Well, maybe we can find something that will point us in the right direction," Valentine suggested.

"It's possible. Any idea where we could start?"

Valentine thought for a moment. "Actually, yeah. If we go to the bio-institute, we can check the data registry. If there's any information on your guy, it'll be there."

The blue-haired woman from the corner table approached Valentine.

"Incoming, on your seven," said Elliot.

Valentine turned to face the woman. She was much shorter than Elliot had expected.

Her hair was closely cut on the sides, but the top of her head was covered in bright-blue hair. When Valentine stood to greet her, she stood as high as his chest.

"I've got a bone to pick with you," she said to Valentine. "You poached my bounty!"

"I didn't poach anything. I was going after him *way* before you were," replied Valentine.

"Well, I still think you owe me a few drinks." She shot Valentine a smile.

"Elliot, this is Blue. She's a demon hunter and expert tracker. Blue, Elliot."

"Nice to meet you." Elliot extended his hand.

"I'm sure," she said, ignoring Elliot's hand. "So what are you two Halloween decorations up to?"

Valentine chuckled. "Showing Elliot the finer parts of the underworld." He ordered her a drink. "Trying to come up with a plan to track someone down."

"Any way I can help?" offered Blue.

"I wish," said Valentine. "Unfortunately, they aren't a demon."

"Who exactly is he?" she asked.

"He's some sort of chemist, I guess. Just trying to help Elliot find him."

"Must be an important guy then."

"He killed my brother," said Elliot, offering up some information.

"Ah, I'm sorry. So, you're stuck with *this* bag of bones, huh?" Blue was trying to change the topic.

"Yeah, he's showing me a few cool tricks. Getting kinda tired of his puns though."

"Hey, if you don't appreciate my puns, then maybe I won't help you," Valentine said sarcastically.

"Depriving the boy of your obnoxious humor, how will he *ever* survive?" humored Blue.

Valentine smiled. "I'll see you around, Blue. Enjoy your drink."

"Oh, I'm sure you will," said Blue, raising her drink toward Valentine.

"All right, because we won't know exactly where we're going inside the institute, we should disguise ourselves so we can move around freely," said Valentine.

"And how do you suggest we do that?" asked Elliot. "Pretty sure we'll easily stand out as irregulars in there."

"That's why we're going to take over someone else's body," replied Valentine.

"*What?*" asked a bewildered Elliot.

"Relax," said Valentine. "It's easier than you think. Stick around here for a bit until you find someone, then meet me at the bar across the street in two hours. We'll go in once it's dark. Got it?"

"Wai—" Elliot started to say, but Valentine vanished.

A couple of hours later, Elliot walked into the bar that Valentine had told him to meet him at. He had found his intended target but wasn't sure what to do next. He was hoping Valentine could help him. He didn't see Valentine inside so he decided to sit at the bar and get himself a drink.

Elliot sat down next to a cute woman with blond hair that curled elegantly around her shoulders. Thin, stylish glasses made her green eyes sparkle in the bar lights.

It had been a long time since Elliot had spoken to a woman he found attractive, and since he had time to kill, he thought he would give it a shot.

"Hi," he said. "I'm Elliot."

The woman blushed and offered her hand. "Serena," she said with a smile. Her voice was as smooth as a summer breeze.

"Can I get you a drink?" Elliot asked.

"I really should be going, but I think I have time for a drink or two."

Elliot ordered two drinks. "Um, I don't mean to come off as weird, but uh, I haven't spoken to a woman in a while, and I get really nervous around attractive women," Elliot said nervously, handing Serena her drink.

"Well, thanks, sweet stuff. You're not too bad yourself," she said in a much more masculine voice.

"*Valentine?*" Elliot was mortified.

Valentine slumped onto the bar in laughter, even pounding his fist on the bar. "You were trying to flirt with me!" Valentine exclaimed.

"What? No! I—"

"Ah, save it." Valentine wiped a tear from his eye. "Why aren't you in disguise?" he asked.

"Well … I, uh, kinda need some help."

Elliot led Valentine outside and opened the trunk of a car. Inside was a middle-aged man, his hands and feet were tied, and he had tape over his mouth. His eyes widened when he saw Elliot, and he let out muffled screams.

"Jesus fucking Christ, Elliot! I said take over their body, not fucking *kidnap* them!" Valentine scolded.

"I didn't know what to do!" Elliot defended himself.

Valentine let out a heavy sigh. With a quick motion, he punched the tied-up man in the face, knocking him out. "Put your hands on his arm and focus your energy into him."

Elliot took hold of the man's arm and closed his eyes. He slowly turned into a black mist that swirled around the man and then seeped into him.

The man's eyes blinked open, and he mumbled.

Valentine removed the tape from his mouth.

"Can you untie me?" Elliot asked.

"Nah, I think I'll leave you in there for now," replied Valentine, closing the trunk.

"Valentine!" Elliot shouted.

Elliot and Valentine made their way through the institute disguised as scientists. The other people in the building paid no attention to them.

"See, told you this would work," said Valentine.

"Still don't know why you left me in that trunk for an hour."

"Sshh. Focus on the task at hand."

The institute was a labyrinth of rooms and corridors. "How the hell are we supposed to find *anything* in here?" Elliot asked.

"We'll have to find some sort of directory," replied Valentine. "Yeah, over here, look." Valentine pointed to a directory next to some elevators. "Registry is in the basement. Of course it is."

"Ah, Doctor Henson! I didn't know you would be working late," came a voice.

Elliot and Valentine turned to see another man in a lab coat behind them.

Valentine nudged Elliot. "I think he means *you*," he whispered.

"Uh—well, you know me. Always so much work to be done," said Elliot.

"Yes, but I've never known you to stay late," said the man.

"It's a … um, a secret project." Elliot wasn't sure he sounded very convincing.

"Hi, I'm the 'secret' project," said Valentine, extending a hand with a wink.

"Bill, you sly dog," the man said with a sheepish grin. "Well, I'll let you, uh, get to your research then." He gave Elliot a wink before walking away.

"What the fuck was that?" asked Elliot.

"Well, I had to say *something*," Valentine replied.

"You're twisted," said Elliot.

The two rode the elevator to the basement and stepped into a gated lobby. Valentine walked over to the ID scanner and ran his badge. The scanner responded with a red flash of light indicating the ID was rejected.

"Here, lemme try." Elliot scanned his ID but received the same red flash. "Did your plan include this?" he asked sarcastically.

"The best plans are ones that can adapt," replied Valentine. He put his hand on the scanner and focused his energy.

The scanner blinked green, and the gate opened.

"Age before beauty," said Valentine, stepping to the side.

"Fuck you," replied Elliot as he walked through the gate.

"Any idea what you're looking for in here?" asked Valentine.

"Terminal access, I guess. I need to run the name through data logs."

"Computer over there." Valentine pointed.

"Perfect. You keep watch, and I'll run the name," said Elliot. He powered up the screen and entered the chemist's name into the data log.

"Hey! No one is supposed to be in here. This is a restricted area!" yelled a security guard.

"Can your plan adapt to *this?*" asked Elliot.

"Relax, I got this," whispered Valentine.

Valentine then took advantage of his persona, trying to distract the guard. "I'm so sorry to intrude. I was just looking for some information that could help me in my research. Perhaps you could help a poor little scientist?"

"Mmm, you really shouldn't be in here. But I suppose you can look, as long as I accompany you."

"Oh, of course," said Valentine. He shot Elliot a wink as he walked out of sight with the guard.

Elliot let out a sigh of relief and continued scanning the data logs.

Valentine returned a few moments later.

"What happened? Where's the guard?" Elliot asked.

"We won't need to worry about him for a while. Find anything yet?"

"I think so. Says here he used to work for a lab called 'Bio-Technika,' and he received some funding for his work in virology."

"Off to Bio-Technika then."

CHAPTER 6

SUBSTANCE 114

The next morning, Valentine and Rebecca sat together in the den of Valentine's farmhouse drinking coffee.

"I'm worried about Elliot." Rebecca held her mug with both hands and took a sip. "He seems like he's got a lot on his mind lately, and, well, there's not a light way to put it, but Matthew's murder is obviously weighing on him."

"It's hard losing someone close to you. Life is fragile, and that realization can take a toll on some," replied Valentine.

Rebecca leaned on Valentine's arm. "Will you go talk to him? He seems more willing to talk to you."

"I'll see what I can do."

Elliot was sitting outside on the patio, staring expressionlessly into the woods beyond the yard.

"Top of the morning," said Valentine, taking a seat beside Elliot. "You look like shit."

"Means a lot comin' from you," Elliot said sarcastically. "I keep seeing Matthew's face every time I close my eyes. I wish I could go back in time. There's so many things I would do over."

"You're not alone," said Valentine. His tone turned from comforting to somber. "Everyone lives with regrets; it's part of being human."

"I just wish I could've spent a few more minutes with him." Elliot bit his lower lip.

"I can sense your hatred for death, but don't let that change into a hatred of life," said Valentine.

"Well, then what's the meaning of it?" Elliot asked.

"The answer is in the question itself. The meaning of life is simply that, to *live*. There's a twisted balance to it all. Without death, all the little things we experience, all those happy and special moments, would lose their meaning. The macabre side of that is, we don't truly know the value of those moments until they're gone. It's only after a moment has passed that we realize the happiness or love that we felt. You may tell yourself you're happy, but even you see through your lies. Only in hindsight can you see the clarity of those moments in the shadow of reality, and you know what true happiness felt like. You have to hold on to those moments; that's what keeps someone alive."

Elliot stayed quiet, listening to Valentine's words.

Valentine fell silent, like he was lost in thought for a moment. "My mom did so much for my brother and me, and it's only when I look back, I see how much she did for us, which ended up costing her life."

Elliot looked at Valentine. He wanted to ask what happened, but didn't know how to do so.

Valentine saw the question in Elliot's face. "I grew up during the Depression. It was hard. My dad ended up walking out and left my mother to care for two small boys. She ... did what she thought she had to do. Selling herself out just to put scraps of food on the table ... One night, I could hear yelling and screaming coming from her room. I could hear my mom sobbing before everything fell silent." Valentine seemed to struggle with the next bit of the story. He choked on his words. "A while later ... a man came out of her room, still tightening his belt. I could see my mom lying motionless on the bed, blood dripping from her mouth ... He ... he killed her."

Valentine's mind flashed back to a fat man with greasy hair, tightening his belt. He put a hand on Valentine's head and ruffled his hair. "Hey, little buddy," the man said to him. Valentine's mind came back to the present. "The things she did for her kids ... that's why I do what I do."

Elliot was at a complete loss for words now but didn't want to leave Valentine hanging in silence. "Did ... did you ever find him?" he finally managed to ask.

Valentine nodded silently. "After the war," he started. "I tracked him down. He was a priest. Did some investigating and turned out he had a history of raping women and children."

"That's fucked up …" Elliot grimaced at the thought.

"So, I went into the confessional booth, and I told him the same story I just told you. Then I confessed to the sin I was about to commit."

Elliot's eyes widened. "What did you do?" he asked.

"I crucified him to the cross above the church organ."

That night, Elliot and Valentine went to Bio-Technika. In the Reaper forms and enrobed in darkness, they made their way inside the building, permeating through the locked doors. The building was vacant of employees, and the halls were dark.

"Any idea what you're looking for here?" asked Valentine, gliding silently down the hallway.

Elliot preferred walking over gliding, and his boots made small thuds with each step. "Archives, I guess. The data at the institute said he was terminated from here after working on a project called 'Green Water.'"

"Any idea what the project was?" Valentine inquired.

"No fuckin' idea," responded Elliot.

They passed several labs along the way to the archives. Valentine peered into windows to see if he could spot anything interesting. "Always thought it would be cool to be a scientist. Imagine all the fascinating things they research here," he said.

"Dunno," replied Elliot, uninterested in the lab's research. "Archives up ahead."

They passed through the door to the archives and entered a large room with what seemed like an endless amount of filing cabinets.

"Guess they prefer the old-fashioned method here," Valentine commented.

"Yeah, not gonna be as easy as I thought." Elliot looked around at all the cabinets. "I don't even know where to start."

"Why don't you look for his name, and I'll look for 'Green Water,'" suggested Valentine.

Elliot nodded his head, and the two split up and went in different directions. Elliot thought he would start by searching for the doctor's last name. He opened the drawer of the "M" files and slowly flicked through the file names. He finally found a tab labeled "Meier," but there was only one paper in the file. Elliot pulled the paper out and looked at it. "A termination letter," he said to himself. He closed the drawer and went off to see if Valentine had made any progress with his search.

Valentine was actually making his way to Elliot with a folder in his hand.

"You found something?" Elliot asked enthusiastically.

"Not much but enough to help us, I think," replied Valentine, handing the file to Elliot.

Elliot opened the folder and scanned through its contents. "Bio research," he said. "Doesn't say what exactly the focus of the research was." Elliot continued reading through the pages. "Meier was partnered with a guy named 'Glen Matsuda' for the duration of the project."

"You see the name when you were flicking through those files?" Valentine asked.

"I found Meier, but I didn't see Matsuda," Elliot answered.

"Could've been outside help," Valentine suggested.

"Or the file could've been stolen," said Elliot. He turned the folder so Valentine could see it and revealed the edges of pages torn from the file. "If someone stole the pages, why didn't they take the *whole* file?"

"Maybe they only needed the important parts." Valentine shrugged.

"If someone stole Matsuda's file, then they could be hunting him down," said Elliot.

"Then we better find him first."

Elliot and Valentine made their way down Queen's Boulevard, the main street in Sterling Heights, a place where the higher-class citizens of Sterling could flaunt their wealth in luxury condos.

"Bex seems to like ya," said Elliot.

"She's nice," replied Valentine.

"You don't like her?" asked Elliot.

"It's not like that."

"What, you scared of commitment or something?" said Elliot, trying to poke fun.

"It's not—" Valentine started to say and then seemingly changed his mind, biting back his words and beginning again. He stopped gliding and turned to Elliot, adding to the seriousness of his answer. "I understand you don't know what it's like, but it's hard being immortal and watching the people you care about die, especially when there's nothing you can do to stop it. It's not that I don't like Bex; I just can't bear to make attachments anymore."

The thought had never occurred to him before, and the sudden realization of it was like someone had slapped him in the face with a brick.

"Warren is all I really have left," added Valentine. He turned and looked up the street. "Condo is right up there. Looking for *4 Emerald Lane*."

The front door of Matsuda's luxury condo was open when Elliot and Valentine got there.

"I really hope he just forgot to close his door," said Elliot.

"I don't think so. Be ready." Valentine drew his sword and pushed the door open with his shoulder before stepping inside.

Elliot drew his sword and followed Valentine.

The inside of the condo looked like it had been ransacked. Drawers were open, and their contents were strewn all over the floor. Chairs were tipped over, and paintings were torn from their hangers and tossed on the floor. Broken glass and laundry littered the floor.

"Looks like someone beat us here," said Valentine.

"They must've been looking for something other than Matsuda," said Elliot.

"Well, judging by the fact that Matsuda is right there, I'd say you're right," said Valentine, pointing to a blood trail that led to Matsuda on the floor of his bedroom.

"Jesus Christ," said Elliot. He rushed over to Matsuda and knelt down. "He's alive but just barely." Elliot gently shook Matsuda. "Hey! Who did this?" Elliot asked him.

Matsuda struggled to speak and choked on his own blood.

"What were they looking for?" asked Elliot.

Still choking on blood, Matsuda was struggling to breathe. He stuck out his bloody clenched fist and placed it into Elliot's bony hand as he closed his eyes for the final time, his last sight that of a ghostly skeleton in black robes.

Elliot took what was in Matsuda's hand and listened to his last breath. "It's a key. There must be a safe in here."

"Let me see the key," said Valentine, taking it from Elliot. "If there was a safe in here, I think our uninvited guests would have found it. This looks like a key to a safety deposit box."

"We need whatever is in that box," said Elliot.

The next morning, Elliot went and tracked down the safety deposit box. After he was escorted to a private room, a gentleman in a suit came in, put a silver box on the table in front of him, and then left the room.

Elliot inserted the key and unlocked the box.

The only thing inside the box was a leather-bound journal.

Back at the farmhouse, Elliot and Valentine were examining the journal.

"Matsuda took notes the entire time he was working on Green Water!" exclaimed Elliot.

"This is amazing," said Valentine. "Look at this right here." He pointed to a page. "Substance *114.*"

Substance 114 is a synthetic virus
<u>HIGHLY UNSTABLE</u>
Special precautions must be taken at all times
So far, all symptoms untreatable, all test subjects
have died within day of exposure to 114
Animal test subject: 187 has developed abscesses
over the whole of its body and has developed
uncontrollable bleeding. Substance is highly fear
dangerous. Effects seem to be similar to that
of the Marburg virus and the flu. The reaper

"This must be what he's after," said Elliot. "Everything on the virus is in Matsuda's journal."

"Does he say what happened to the project?"

"Says here funding was revoked, and the project was shut down after Meier used a human test subject without approval from the board. So *that's* why Meier was terminated."

"You think he might be back in operation?"

"I saw one of his operations firsthand," replied Elliot.

Valentine paced around the room for a moment. "I want to help you," he started to say.

"But?" asked Elliot.

"No buts," replied Valentine. "If you would let me finish, I was going to ask if you could give me the full story of what exactly happened on that island."

"Ah," said Elliot. "Can we take this conversation outside?"

"Of course," Valentine replied. He paged Warren and asked him to bring a bottle of scotch to the firepit outside.

Valentine lit the fire and pulled up two chairs. He poured them each a glass of scotch. "Start when you're ready," he said to Elliot, handing him a glass.

"It was spring break," said Elliot, taking a sip of scotch. "I was a, uh, a history major. Decided to use that time to go exploring in the Pacific islands and study culture. Somewhere over the ocean, the plane went down. Me and like eight other people survived the crash and all washed up on some island." Elliot took another sip of his drink. "First people we encountered turned out to be a cannibal tribe of natives."

"Sounds like a hell of a vacation so far," said Valentine, lighting a joint of malice.

"Oh, it was," replied Elliot. "Despite the crash-landing and being chased by cannibals."

Valentine chuckled.

"There were these mercenaries on the island, and they were kidnapping natives from the island and putting them on a ship. I ended up helping some people escape from their cages on the beach but didn't make it too far." Elliot took the joint from Valentine and took a drag.

"Then what?"

Elliot pointed to a long scar on the left side of his head. "Took a shot to the head. Luckily, it just grazed me, but, uh, I stumbled off a cliff, I'm pretty sure." He took another drag and then handed it back to Valentine. "When I came to, I was in some sort of massive village. They treated my wounds and taught me how to sword fight."

"So where does Meier come in?" asked Valentine.

"If you would let me finish," Elliot mocked. "This other village was being ransacked by the mercs, and we went to help. Only, guns are better than swords. They took most of us as prisoners and put us on that ship and locked us up. Treated us like animals. Meier was using prisoners as human test subjects for different experiments. Eventually, we made a plan to break free and take control of the ship."

"Did it work?"

Elliot shook his head. "Meier had the whole thing rigged with explosives." Elliot finished the rest of his drink in one big sip. "We need to find this fucker."

CHAPTER 7

THE PLAGUE

Valentine was drinking coffee in the den, watching the news when Elliot came in.

"Y'know, I miss sleeping," said Elliot.

"Try meditating," replied Valentine, taking a sip of coffee.

"Anything interesting?" asked Elliot, looking at the TV.

"New flu going around. At least you don't have to worry about shots anymore," Valentine said cheerfully.

Elliot nodded. "Any coffee left?"

"Drank it all." Valentine raised his mug toward Elliot. "Cheers."

Elliot was unamused. "Guess I'll make some more then."

"Hold that thought," said Valentine. "Let's go get something to eat. I know this great little dive on the west side called Limbo's."

"The *west* side?" Elliot asked.

"What, you scared you're going to get shot?"

Elliot shrugged. Valentine made a fair point. It's not like they had much to be scared of now.

Police sirens wailed in the distance as Elliot and Valentine entered the diner. The diner was a popular dining spot for gangs on the west side of the city, and the patrons all looked at Elliot and Valentine as they went to their table, but Valentine paid no mind to them.

"Why do you wear a suit everywhere? You look like a trust-fund baby," remarked Elliot.

"Well, you look like a sewer dweller who lives in a shoebox, you ten-piece McNobody," replied Valentine, gesturing to Elliot's baggy sweater and ripped jeans. Valentine gave a sheepish grin.

"You're gonna get robbed in a place like this," said Elliot.

"Well then, I guess it's a good thing I eat here for free." Valentine flagged a waitress with his hand. "I like wearing suits. Reminds me of a different time," he said to Elliot.

"Hey, Val!" came an angelic voice.

Valentine smiled at the waitress and admired her blond curls and ruby-red lips. "Good morning, Astrid."

"Coffee and orange juice?" asked Astrid, pulling a notepad and pen from her apron pocket. "And to eat, French toast with a side of bacon?"

"You know me so well," replied Valentine with a smile.

"Gotta keep my favorite guest happy," she said, returning the smile.

"Can I also get a coffee and orange juice?" asked Elliot, cutting into the romance.

"Of course, and to eat?" asked Astrid, her eyes still on Valentine.

"A Western, please," replied Elliot, unsure if the waitress even heard him.

"Be right back." Astrid gave a little wave to Valentine as she walked away.

"That was gross to watch," said Elliot.

Valentine smiled. "Shut up."

"*Val?* What was that?"

"She's just being nice," Valentine replied.

"Well, I can see why this is your favorite place now."

"The food is good too." Valentine grinned.

Astrid returned with the drinks and set them on the table. "Be back in a bit."

"She gave me apple juice," said Elliot.

"Sucks to suck," replied Valentine, taking a big gulp of orange juice.

A chair scraped loudly on the ground, and there was a clatter of dishes and utensils followed by a "thud" and several people gasping.

People in the diner circled around a man writhing on the ground in pain. He scratched at his chest as his eyes rolled into the back of his head.

Valentine rushed to the man and knelt by his side, observing the man's condition. "Elliot, call an ambulance!" he commanded.

That night, in their Reaper forms, Valentine took Elliot to the top of a building.

"What are we doing here?" asked Elliot.

"Meeting someone," replied Valentine, looking up at the sky. "When I was a kid, you could still see the stars in the sky. Can't see anything now."

The metal rooftop door creaked as it opened. Elliot put his right hand on his left sword, but Valentine silently stuck out his hand and stopped him.

Valentine turned to face the footsteps approaching from behind him. "What did you find?" he asked.

A middle-aged, spectacled man with well-kept hair and wearing a doctor's coat stood before them. "I, uh … wasn't expecting *two* of you." His voice was shaky and nervous.

"What did you find?" Valentine repeated, ignoring the man's comment.

"It's not a flu," he said, handing Valentine a manila folder.

Valentine opened the folder and flicked through its contents with a bony finger.

"We think it's some sort of toxin, but we can't identify what it is," said the doctor.

Valentine nodded his head silently as he read the papers. He closed the folder and handed it back to the doctor.

"You can keep that. I made you a copy," the doctor said.

"Very well," replied Valentine.

"Oh, I, uh, we also found these in the pocket of the man you mentioned this morning." The doctor handed Valentine a bag of small green capsules.

"What is this?"

"We, uh, I don't know," the doctor replied, bowing his head to avoid eye contact with Valentine. "They were found in one of the patient's pockets. We sent out a dose for testing, but the lab results were confiscated."

"Who did you send it out to?" Valentine asked.

"Bio-Technika," the doctor replied.

Valentine removed a capsule and handed it to the doctor. "Test one. Keep it in-house."

The following morning

"What are your thoughts on the pills?" asked Elliot. He took a sip of coffee and then leaned back in his chair.

Valentine was looking out a window to his right. "We have to find a way of testing its chemical formula," he replied, turning to face Elliot.

"Think it could be the work of Meier?"

"Could be, but the only way of knowing is to test it." Valentine took a sip of coffee and then rested the mug on his lap.

"Got any connections?" Elliot asked.

Valentine shook his head no.

"You're telling me the one person who knows everyone doesn't know a chemist?" Elliot said sarcastically.

"Nope. But if you need a taxidermist or a belly dancer, I can give you some names." Valentine put his mug on the table and then leaned back in his chair, interlocking his fingers behind his head.

"Do you think Bio-Tech would have the lab results?" asked Elliot.

Valentine sighed as he thought. "I doubt it. They probably don't want anything pointing back to them."

"Don't suppose you could test it yourself?" Elliot suggested.

"Do I look like a chemist?" Valentine asked rhetorically, while gesturing to himself.

"S'cuse me, boys. Couldn't help but overhear your conversation," said Warren.

Elliot's eyes widened, and he gave Valentine a concerned look.

Valentine held up a hand and gave Elliot a look that said, "Relax. He knows."

"My grandson is in the science program at his college. I could give him a ring," Warren suggested.

Valentine looked at Elliot. "Not a bad idea."

"Don't really have any other options," Elliot replied.

"If you can set something up with your grandson, that would be great," Valentine told Warren.

"I'll ring him up and give you the lowdown," Warren replied before shuffling out of the kitchen.

"That settles that then. Time for a drink," said Valentine, raising his eyebrows.

"At ten in the morning?" asked Elliot, glancing at the clock.

"Time is no longer relevant when you can't die," Valentine said sarcastically as he poured vodka into orange juice. He raised his glass toward Elliot with a sheepish grin before taking a large sip.

That night, Elliot and Valentine met Warren's grandson, Ethan, at Walker University. Valentine wore a casual gray suit, and Elliot was in his usual sweater and jeans.

"Thanks for helping us," said Valentine, shaking Ethan's hand.

"Hey, anything for my grandfather. Didn't know he had such young friends," Ethan commented. He was a young, freckled man with disheveled hair and wore a stained lab coat. He carried himself with a sort of ambiguous eccentricity and would prove to have no respect for personal boundaries.

"He's a good man. Has a lot of interesting stories to tell," said Valentine, trying to avoid any personal topics.

"Does he tell you about the war?" Ethan asked. "Man, I wish I could get him to open up about that. Has he ever killed anybody?"

This kid is in the wrong major, Valentine thought to himself. "Uh, no, he doesn't talk about the war much. Listen, I was hoping you could test something for us." Valentine was trying to get the conversation back on track.

"Right, right. Whatcha got?"

Valentine handed the bag of bright-green pills to Ethan. "Need you to find out what's inside these."

"Yeah, all right, I can do that, no problem," Ethan replied. "So, like, are you guys in pharmaceuticals or detectives?" He began adding drops of various liquids to a beaker with the contents of the pills, observing them as they bubbled and foamed.

Elliot gave Valentine a look that said, "Well?"

Valentine was growing tired of Ethan's personal questions and incessant talking. "Yeah, pharmaceuticals. We're looking to expand our industry and wanted to see what the new equipment was like." Time to change the topic again. "So what did your grandfather do in the war?"

Ethan had his back turned to Elliot and Valentine and was busy with his work but was still eager to talk about the war. "Oh! He was a rifleman!" he replied excitedly, his eyes still focused on his craft. "Went all the way through Europe," he added.

A machine started to buzz as it spit out a sheet of paper.

Ethan took the paper and read it over before handing it to Valentine.

Valentine took the paper and held it up so Elliot could also view it.

"Twelve percent fentanyl, traces of glyphosate, tabun, ammonia, and cocaine. A majority of it though is made up of some sort of unknown substance; it's not in any of our records," said Ethan.

Valentine handed the paper to Elliot.

"So, uh, where'd you guys get this stuff exactly? Pretty deadly shit," Ethan remarked.

Fuck, Valentine thought to himself. If it was any other person, he would simply banish them to the darkness. But he couldn't do that to Warren's grandson. "It's from a competitor. We, uh … found it." He traded glances with Elliot.

"You've been a big help. We'll tell Warren how great you are," said Elliot quickly, trying to keep Ethan from talking.

Elliot and Valentine left as quickly as they could to avoid any further questioning from Ethan.

"Jesus, felt like I was being interrogated in there," said Elliot once outside.

"Yeah, no kidding," Valentine replied.

"He sure talked a lot," Elliot commented.

"Yeah," said Valentine, his mind somewhat adrift.

"So, what now?" Elliot asked. "Gotta find out where they're making this stuff."

Valentine ran a hand through his hair. "Could try to buy some more." His phone rang. "Hello?"

After a short conversation, Valentine put his phone away.

"Who was that?" asked Elliot.

"The doctor we met with last night."

"What'd he want?"

"The guy with the pills died. They also have a dozen more patients with the same symptoms."

"Did anyone else have anything on them indicating poison?" Elliot inquired.

"No," answered Valentine. "It seems it's spreading like a flu."

CHAPTER 8

THE OLD MILLS

Valentine donned his black robes and waited on the roof of the hospital. The smoke that clung to his cloak danced in the breeze.

The metal door of the roof access opened with a creak and closed with a metallic thud.

"Ah, you're alone this time," the doctor said.

Valentine turned his back on the city to face the doctor. "What do you have for me?" he asked.

The doctor nervously put his hands in the pockets of his lab coat. "Several more patients have been admitted showing the same symptoms as the man you inquired about."

"To what extent are the symptoms?"

"Head and body aches, fevers and chills, fatigue, chest tightness along with stomach pains and nausea. All flu-like symptoms," the doctor replied. "Though we have a couple patients under intensive watch who are experiencing hysteria and seizures." The doctor waited anxiously for Valentine to reply. "I fear we may have a pandemic on our hands," he added.

"It's no flu," replied Valentine. "Toxicology reports?" he asked.

"Right here," the doctor replied, handing Valentine another folder. "They all had the same chemicals in their system."

"A little too coincidental for a pandemic, don't you think? These people are being poisoned," Valentine replied as he flipped through the papers.

"Poisoned?" the doctor asked in astonishment. "With what? What should we do to treat them?" he asked Valentine.

"How should I know? *You're* the doctor," Valentine replied sternly.

"Doctor offer any useful information?" Elliot asked.

"Nothing we don't already know," replied Valentine. He took a long drag of malice before handing it to Elliot. "We need to find him before he poisons the whole city."

Elliot detected a sense of worry in Valentine's voice. "Any idea where to go from here?" He thought for a moment. "Wait … What if we go with your idea?"

"What was my idea?" Valentine asked.

"We *buy* drugs!" replied Elliot.

Valentine thought for a moment. "We find a seller; then we find out where they get it from."

"So, where exactly do we go to buy drugs?" Elliot asked.

"Jesus, you sound like a cop. Better let me do the talking," said Valentine.

Valentine brought Elliot to an alley on the west side of the city.

"Best ditch our current appearance," Valentine said as the dark smoke swirled around him. Flesh covered his bones, and his dark cloak had taken the shape of a black hooded sweatshirt.

Elliot copied Valentine and changed his appearance. "Are we always visible as a Reaper?" he asked Valentine.

"Yeah, so best to avoid being seen as one lest you want to scare the shit out of people," he replied. He stepped out of the alley and into the street. "Follow me," he told Elliot.

Elliot followed Valentine down the street for a few blocks before they crossed and went down another street. "Where exactly are we going?" he asked.

"You'll see. We're almost there." Valentine led Elliot to a small corner store. They walked around to the rear of the building, and Valentine sat on a brick wall. Lighting a cigarette, he motioned for Elliot to take a seat on the wall as well. "Here," he said, handing Elliot a cigarette.

"I don't smoke," said Elliot, holding a hand up to protest the cigarette.

"Neither do I," replied Valentine. "Just do it."

Two hooded men approached Elliot and Valentine.

"Wus good?" one of them asked, nodding his head at Valentine.

"Fuckin' livin' the dream and hopin' I don't wake up," Valentine replied with a grin.

The man chuckled. "That's wussup. You lookin' ta score?"

"Got any molly?" Valentine asked.

"Nah, man. Got somethin' better." The man pulled out a bag of green pills. "Thirty a pop and you'll be set for the day."

"I think I've heard of these. You know anything about them?" Valentine inquired.

"Nah, man. I just sell," the man replied.

"What if I wanted to move some weight?" Valentine asked, pulling a wad of cash from his pocket.

The man grinned. "Now we talkin'."

The two sketchy men escorted Elliot and Valentine to an apartment building that looked like it hadn't been maintenanced in the last decade. When they got to the door, one of the men knocked on the door four times and paused before knocking two more times. After a series of clinking locks, the door opened.

The two men led Elliot and Valentine upstairs to a room with music playing loudly. Men with guns sat on a couch and watched topless women dance in the center of the room. The man knocked on another door before leading them into another room in the back.

One of the men escorting the duo walked to a man sitting behind a desk and whispered something to him before walking away.

"Come in! Sit!" boomed the man behind the desk.

Elliot and Valentine both sat themselves in leather office chairs in front of the desk.

"My men tell me you are in da moving business," the big man said.

Valentine nodded his head.

"Well, you have come to da right place. But I expect you to pay all up front. I do not do loans."

Valentine put three large wads of cash on the desk.

The man behind the desk smiled wide, revealing two rows of gold teeth. "So, what are you looking for?"

"Right down to business then," said Valentine.

"I am a man of business. I do not like wasting valuable time. So?"

"Lookin' to score some of those green pills."

"Ah, the olives! You are a man of keen taste. I can give you …" The man behind the desk shuffled through the cash in front of him. "Three quarta' pound."

"Deal," said Valentine, extending his hand.

The man took Valentine's hand and shook it. Then he swept the cash into a drawer. He made a motion to one of his men who left and then returned a few moments later carrying a package wrapped in plastic.

"Your green olives," said the big man, gesturing to the plastic-wrapped brick.

"Any idea where these come from?" asked Valentine.

"I do not divulge such information. My business relies on discretion," replied the man. "Especially to new buyers such as yourself."

"Understandable." Valentine glanced at Elliot and winked. With a strong kick, he launched the desk into the man's rib cage. He leaped over the desk and tackled the man out of his chair.

Elliot kicked his chair backward and rolled across the floor. With a quick lunge, he drew his sword and impaled the man by the door.

"Keep that door closed!" Valentine yelled.

Elliot extended his hands and focused his energy on the door. Black smoke formed around the door frame and kept the door closed as men pounded on it from the other side.

Valentine struck the big man in the face. He embraced his Reaper form, and the big man watched in horror as the flesh melted from Valentine's face. "Where are the pills coming from?" he demanded, wrapping both his hands around the man's gargantuan neck.

The man choked and gasped for air as Valentine strangled him. "The … old … mills," he choked out. "A man who lives on the docks."

Valentine picked the man up and slammed him onto the desk. He drew his sword, and in one fluid motion, he decapitated the man. Flesh and blood sizzled from the immense heat of the blade. "Ready to fight our way out?" he asked Elliot.

"Ready when you are," Elliot replied. He had transformed into his Reaper form as well.

Valentine opened a drawer in the desk and took his money back. Then he grabbed the brick of pills and pushed it into a small pouch that hung from his belt.

"How the fuck did that fit?" Elliot asked.

"Another time. Ready?" Valentine drew his sword.

Elliot drew both of his swords. "Ready," he replied.

With a nod from Valentine, Elliot kicked the door open with such force that it knocked down the men who were standing behind it.

Before the men could get back on their feet, Elliot was already upon them. Swinging his swords in furious and fluid motions, he was sending body parts and trails of blood all over the room.

A man fired a machine gun at Elliot, but the bullets passed through him without harm.

Elliot turned to face the man. He extended his left hand, and a mass of darkness shot forward and launched the man into a wall, killing him.

Valentine made his way around Elliot and shot a black mass at a group of men who were coming up the stairs. All of them fell to the floor, dead. "Let's go!" he called to Elliot, leaping over the heap of bodies at the foot of the stairs. As he opened the front door, two more thugs burst in. Grabbing the shotgun the first man was holding, Valentine thrust the butt of it into the man's gut, causing him to bend over winded. He yanked the weapon upward, tearing it from the man's hands and hitting him in the jaw. Valentine spun the shotgun around and shot the second man in the torso before turning the barrel on the first man.

Gunshots rang through the streets, and Elliot and Valentine exited the apartment building.

Valentine's police radio chirped with a staticky voice. "All units, we have reports of multiple shots fired in Downtown West. Possible gang-related violence. All units are requested for immediate response."

"Ugh!" snorted Valentine. "Let's see if we can clean this up before Sterling's *finest* show up," he told Elliot. "And let's try not to leave a mess for 'em." He extended his hand and ripped weapons from the hands of three men. With his other hand, he hoisted them into the air and tossed them into the back of a box truck before closing and locking the doors.

Elliot moved swiftly across the street and used his powers to push a group of men against a wall, rendering them unconscious.

The duo worked quickly trying to disarm the thugs as police sirens grew louder and louder.

When the police finally arrived on the scene, Elliot and Valentine were gone.

"So, off to the mills?" Elliot suggested.

"And what, walk around all night checking every building?" Valentine said sarcastically.

"Oh, yeah, right. Sorry, forgot I was talking to the world's smartest person," replied Elliot, playing on the sarcasm. "So I suppose you have an idea then?"

"I do, actually. But apparently you're too good for my ideas."

"Oh my fuck, just spit it out," insisted Elliot.

"The mills have been abandoned for around twenty years, yes?"

"Go on …" Elliot made a circling motion with his hands.

"We check the local power grid and see which building is drawing power," Valentine suggested.

"Well, lead the way then, Einstein," said Elliot, waving his hand.

"Don't worry, little guy. Maybe when you're older, you'll start having ideas too," said Valentine, trying to pat Elliot on the head.

"Oh fuck off!" replied Elliot, slapping Valentine's hand away.

"God, you two sound like a married couple," came a familiar voice.

Blue was standing behind them and had overheard their conversation.

"What are you doing here?" asked Elliot.

"I work the corner," she said sarcastically. "I'm chasing a bounty, dipshit." She turned to Valentine. "What are you spooks up to?"

"Still trying to find that chemist," Valentine told her.

"Fuck, you guys are slow. Better hope a bounty doesn't come up on him; otherwise, I'll beat ya to him," Blue bragged.

"Hey, if you can lead us to him, then by all means," replied Valentine, motioning with his hands for her to lead the way.

"Ah, I don't care about your chemist. Got my own tail to chase," said Blue.

"What's the bounty?" Elliot asked.

"A demon that invades people's dreams and eats them," replied Blue.

"Well, we're off to find a power station. You're welcome to join us," Valentine offered.

"Y'know, as fun as that sounds, I'm gonna pass. Catch you ghouls later."

"Y'know, don't particularly care for Blue," Elliot said to Valentine as they made their way to a power station."

"I'll admit, she's a bit of an acquired taste, and her personality is fiery, but she's always had my back when it counted," Valentine replied, defending Blue.

"How'd you two meet anyway?" Elliot asked.

"Believe it or not, I was one of her bounties a ways back."

"Oh, wow, someone wanted you dead? I believe it. So what happened?"

"The client took out a bounty on Blue as well, double-crossed her. Was kind of a scratch-each-other's-back-type of situation. She's been haunting me ever since," Valentine regaled him. He climbed the stairs to the power station and phased through the door. After accessing a computer, he pulled up a view of the local electrical grid. "Hmm, guess our little *friend* was telling the truth."

"See anything out of the ordinary?" asked Elliot.

"That's one way of putting it. Look at this building right here next to the old river port," said Valentine, pointing at the computer screen.

"What about it?" Elliot asked.

"This building here is drawing low amounts of energy," Valentine explained.

"So what's it powering? Can't be enough to power a whole lab," said Elliot.

"Could be a number of things," said Valentine. "A fridge, a generator, maybe a small transceiver. Fuck if I know. Only one way to find out though."

"Hey!" a voice called behind them. "You're not supposed to be in here."

The duo turned around to see a substation employee standing in the doorway.

Before the man could say anything more, Valentine waved his hand, and the man collapsed on the floor and began snoring. "Time to go," said Valentine.

Elliot and Valentine stood on a rotting dock at the old river port.

"This whole place used to be thriving, once upon a time. I remember when this port was still being used," said Valentine, talking mostly to himself but also to Elliot.

"Long time ago," said Elliot.

Valentine nodded. "Laid off a lot of workers during the Depression. Then, when the war broke out, the women made bullets, planes, and tanks here."

"A lot of history here."

"Indeed," replied Valentine. He produced a silver pocket watch from his cloak and checked the time. "Two hours before sunrise. Better make this quick," he said, putting his watch away.

"This the one?" asked Elliot, pointing at a rundown mill building with smashed windows.

"Yessir. I'll take the lead. Follow me," instructed Valentine. He approached the building and peered in through some of the windows.

"See anything?" Elliot asked.

"No. Let's head inside," replied Valentine. He drew his sword and phased through the door.

Elliot followed suit.

The building was dusty, dark, and empty.

"There's no one here," said Elliot.

"Great observation, Sherlock," remarked Valentine, sheathing his sword. "Looks like someone may have been here recently though." He pointed at footprints in the dust. "Looks like four different sets, by my count."

"Mmm, and it looks like some of the stuff in here has been dragged across the floor as well.

Valentine was following the footprints to the other side of the building. Ahead of him, he could see something on the ground.

Elliot, meanwhile, was following drag marks that looked like they were made from a large crate. He followed the tracks to a door and opened it.

A wire tied to the door stretched as Elliot opened it. There was a faint "beep" followed by an explosion that hurled fire through the whole building. The roof and walls began to collapse from the heat and fire. The whole building collapsed within minutes with a massive crash as flames and smoke bellowed into the air.

"You just *had* to blow the place up, huh?" said Valentine, in an irritated and sarcastic tone.

Elliot, at a loss for words, shrugged his shoulders. "Whoops."

"Can't take you anywhere."

CHAPTER 9

MISTAKES

Back in their human forms, Elliot and Valentine went to the diner on the west side.

"I didn't know the door was rigged," said Elliot, picking up a menu. "I was just trying to follow the tracks," he added.

"I get that part, but why the fuck did you open the door? When have you ever seen me open a door?" Valentine scolded.

"All right, fair point," Elliot conceded. "Did you at least find what was drawing the electricity?" he asked.

"I *would* have if you didn't blow the place up first."

Before Elliot could reply, Astrid came to the table. "Hey, you!" she said to Valentine. "Wow, you guys smell like a chimney. Beer?"

"That would be wonderful. Actually ..." Valentine looked at his watch. "Coffee, please."

"And you?"

"Same," replied Elliot.

"Be right back with those," said Astrid, giving a little wave to Valentine.

"Why are we here?" asked Elliot.

"Because I'm hungry," replied Valentine.

"You get blown up, and your first reaction is to get something to eat?"

"Listen, I was already hungry; it's not my fault *you* blew me up."

Astrid brought the coffees back and placed them on the table. "The usual?" she asked Valentine.

Valentine nodded with a smile.

Astrid turned to Elliot to take his order but didn't say anything.

"Uh, same, I guess?" said Elliot.

"You want to see what I found?" Valentine asked after Astrid left.

"Let's see it," replied Elliot.

Valentine slid a piece of paper with singed edges across the table.

Elliot picked it up and looked at it. "It's an address," he said.

"Cain Enterprises," said Valentine.

"I don't understand," replied Elliot, studying the paper.

"Makes two of us," said Valentine.

"Think it belongs to Meier?" Elliot asked.

"Or his mercenary pet," added Valentine.

"What do you think they're after?"

"Cain fills military contracts for weapons and targeting systems, optics, explosive ordinance, experimental shit. Take your pick."

"Do they deal with chemicals? Or bio-technology?" asked Elliot.

"Hell if I know. Cain Enterprises isn't known for sharing secrets."

Astrid brought large stacks of pancakes and put them on the table. "Enjoy," she said with a smile.

Elliot couldn't help but notice a much larger portion of bacon on Valentine's plate. "Flirt with the waitress for extra bacon?" he asked.

Valentine chortled. "A kind word can get you many things. We'll swing by Cain after we're finished eating and have a chat with security." He drowned his plate in syrup. "I must commend you," he said, slicing into his breakfast.

"For?" asked Elliot, mixing cream and sugar into his coffee.

"You've come a long way so far," replied Valentine, his mouth full of food. "Didn't think you'd last as a Reaper."

"I'm still not thrilled with the idea," Elliot replied, staring into his coffee. "If anything … I'm doing this for Matthew."

"Any luck?" asked Elliot, leaning against his car.

Valentine was walking back from Cain Enterprises. "Biometric scanners, infrared lasers, ambient temperature monitors, even particle scanners that monitor air movement. Even *we* would have a hard time getting in there quietly," he said, leaning against the car next to Elliot.

"They mention anything that someone might be liable to steal?" Elliot inquired.

"Whole place is filled with high-tech gizmos. Everything in there is potentially worth stealing."

"So what now?"

"I could use a snack," Valentine replied.

"Dude, you literally *just* ate. What is it with you and food?"

"What is it with you and being such a Debbie Downer?" Valentine retorted.

Their argument was interrupted by a sudden explosion at the top of Cain Enterprises that rained down smoldering debris on the streets below.

Valentine waved his arm, summoning a black dome that shielded him and Elliot from the debris.

"Meier," Elliot said coldly.

"Let's get up there, quick," said Valentine, donning his black cloak and ghostly appearance.

Elliot and Valentine quickly reached the upper floors of the building and found Cain security outnumbered and outgunned.

Men in black uniforms and helmets carrying rifles were making their way through the rooms and halls, firing at the security.

"Those are Novak's men. I recognize the insignia," Elliot told Valentine.

"Guess they also figured they couldn't come in here quietly." Valentine moved over to a security guard crouched behind a tipped desk, pistol in hand. "We're here to help. We'll clear a path for you and your men to follow," Valentine told the man.

He nodded silently and waved to some of the other guards.

Valentine leaped over the desk and attacked the first mercenary he saw. Grabbing the man by the helmet, Valentine threw him out of one of the upper-story windows.

Two other men who heard their comrade scream turned and fired their rifles at Valentine.

Valentine advanced on the men as the bullets passed through him with no damage. He drew his sword, and with a spinning motion with the blade, he sliced through the rifles that the men were holding and rendered them useless. Extending his free hand, with an unseen force, he lifted the two men off the ground. They kicked their legs and clawed at their throats as if being suffocated. Valentine clenched his fist, and there were two simultaneous snaps. The men stopped moving, and Valentine opened his fist, dropping the lifeless bodies to the floor.

Elliot was clearing a path down another hallway, impaling one man with his left sword and severing another man's hands with his right sword and then kicking him in the center of the chest. More mercenaries advanced on him. Elliot pulled his swords close and braced himself.

Elliot stabbed the first man with both of his swords, ripped the rifle from his hands, and shot the other two men. He picked up his swords and sheathed them and then tossed the rifle to one of the security guards.

"What's on this floor?" Valentine asked the security.

"There's nothing on this floor except offices," the guard replied. "But two floors below us is where they develop chemical containment and ordinance."

"In other words?" Elliot asked.

"Warheads," the guard replied in a serious tone.

"You lead your men to safety," Valentine directed the head guard. "We'll take care of this."

"Negative, we're going with you," the guard replied.

When the group reached the intended floor, they found the first hall to be empty. They moved quietly into a larger room dedicated to warhead design.

There was a series of several small metallic "clinks" followed by accompanying "pops" as smoke started to fill the room they were in.

Gunfire broke out all around them. The security guards aimed for the muzzle flashes in the smoke.

"I can't see shit!" Elliot said to Valentine.

"Reach out with the Reaper, and let it be your eyes," Valentine instructed.

Elliot concentrated and reached out with the Reaper. It was like an unseen hand guiding him and showing him his surroundings, revealing what was concealed by smoke. Stepping forward, he drew one of his swords and cut off a mercenary's arm. He followed the swing by thrusting the sword into the man's back and through his chest. Elliot ripped his sword from the man's body, sending a stream of blood through the air.

Another mercenary raised his rifle and fired at two security guards who had a blind eye to him.

Elliot, sensing this, quickly glided across the floor effortlessly and moved in the line of fire with the intention of saving the guards. The bullets passed through Elliot, leaving no damage in their wake. Elliot turned to see that the bullets passed straight through and struck the guards behind him. Realizing his failure to save the men, he turned to the mercenary and dove at him with a burning fury. He thrust both of his swords into the man's midsection and ripped the blades in opposite directions, slicing the mercenary in two and leaving him in a pool of his own blood.

Valentine glided forward silently, and reaching out with his senses, he could detect a group of mercenaries. He extended his hand and focused his power to lift the men off the ground. With his other hand, he used the Reaper's power to shatter a window. Swinging his arm, he tossed the group of men out the window.

A loud alarm sounded, and red lights flashed on the walls.

"They've accessed the containment room!" shouted the head security guard. "Move forward!" he commanded the remaining guards, who accompanied him.

There was a blinding flash followed by a loud "boom" as the floor beneath them collapsed, sending the guards hurtling to the floor below.

Among the sounds of guns firing and the fire roaring, there was the sound of helicopter blades thumping in the wind. The mercenaries quickly retreated and left on the helicopters that had flown up to the side of the building.

Failing to stop the mercenaries, Valentine turned his attention to the security guards who had fallen through the floor.

Of the five men who had fallen, four of them had died from their injuries, including the head guard. The fifth man was alive but unconscious, and he had a large gash on his leg and a bullet wound in his left shoulder.

Scooping the man into his arms, Valentine brought him outside to the emergency responders who were collected around the building. He returned to the building and found Elliot standing among the flames, staring at the bodies of the guards he had tried to shield.

The fire was spreading quickly throughout the building, and Valentine had deduced that the mercenaries had gotten what they came for.

"We-I fucked ..." said Elliot, still looking at the bodies.

"I know how you feel. I went through something similar once." Valentine sighed. "If we can stop Meier, they won't have died for nothing."

Elliot stood in cold silence, replaying the moment over in his head.

"Let's get out of here," said Valentine, placing a bony hand on Elliot's shoulder.

CHAPTER 10

HINDSIGHT

Elliot was sitting outside on the patio as the sun rose, reflecting on the events of the night before. He wished he had been able to stop the mercenaries and prevent so many deaths.

Valentine came outside and took a seat adjacent to Elliot, extending a mug in his direction.

"I don't want coffee," said Elliot, holding up a hand.

"Who said it was coffee?" replied Valentine.

Elliot took the cup and looked into it. "Booze?" he asked.

Valentine smiled in response and took a sip of his own drink.

"Little early, don't ya think?" remarked Elliot.

"Just drink it," Valentine insisted.

"Last night was a fuck-fest."

Valentine nodded. "Yeah … yeah, it was," he said quietly.

Elliot put his drink down. "I'm gonna go for a walk. I'll catch ya later."

Valentine raised his cup but said nothing. He sat back in his chair and admired the view of the rising sun from the patio.

Elliot walked aimlessly down the busy streets of Sterling City, a bustling metropolis that boasted a population of close to nine million people.

The streets were shadowed by large buildings and neon signs and billboards. People walked ignorantly in their own worlds as they went about their business, paying no attention to the others around them. Performers or amateur entertainers could be found on almost every corner.

Elliot bought himself a dark coffee and sat on a bench outside to watch the traffic. When he was much younger, he would sit on the sidewalk with Matthew and listen to him name all the cars that they saw. In fact, Elliot was pretty sure he and Matthew had sat on that same bench together when they were kids. He could almost sense Matthew sitting next to him, and if he closed his eyes and concentrated enough, he could almost hear his voice in the passing cars.

To Elliot, what happened next almost seemed to happen in slow motion. To his left was a large truck barreling down the street. To his right was a woman crossing an intersection, pushing two children in a twin stroller. The traffic lights were red, but the truck showed no signs of stopping, the driver blaring his horn as he approached the crosswalk.

Elliot stood up, knocking his coffee to the ground and spilling it on the concrete. He rushed to the side of the road and called on the Reaper's powers. He extended his hand and, with an unseen force, pushed the truck off course from colliding with the woman.

The truck tires screeched as it came to a stop after hopping the opposite curb and crashing into a building.

Elliot stood stunned for a moment and then quickly looked around to see if anyone had noticed him, but all eyes were fixed on the truck. Elliot rushed toward the woman to see if she was okay but was distracted by a group of people who were gathered around where the truck had collided. Elliot walked toward the group and pushed his way through the crowd but was mortified when he reached the front. He had saved the woman and her two children, but he had inadvertently caused the truck to crash into a man and a woman who were dining outside, killing them instantly.

Elliot felt sick to his stomach and pushed his way back through the crowd. Ducking into an alley, he braced himself against the wall of a building and vomited. "What have I done?" he muttered to himself as the sound of his blood pumping filled his ears.

"Hey, you hear about this?" said Valentine as Elliot walked through the door of the farmhouse. Valentine gestured to the television. "Truck crashed on Main Street, killing two people."

Elliot grabbed the remote, turned the TV off, and then walked outside to the patio.

"I was watching that!" Valentine called out. He decided to follow Elliot outside. "What's going on? You all right?" he asked.

Elliot pursed his lips and shook his head, twirling his hands together. "I caused that accident," he finally said in a remorseful tone. "I … I didn't even see them."

"Wait … *What?* Back up. What happened?" Valentine asked, a puzzled look on his face.

"I was there when it happened," Elliot started. "Woman was crossing the street with her two kids … I thought … I thought I could push the truck out of the way …"

Connecting the dots, Valentine's puzzled look turned to one of empathy. He took a seat next to Elliot. "I-I know it may not mean much right now, but those kids have a whole life ahead of them now, thanks to you," he said, trying to comfort Elliot.

"But what about the people I killed? What about the lives ahead of *them?*" Elliot put his head into his hands and propped his elbows on his legs. "I should've just moved them out of the way. Why the fuck did I push the truck?"

"Everyone fucks up, Elliot. God knows I have," said Valentine.

"You don't even believe in God," replied Elliot.

"That's not the point. Point is, I've fucked up too, and sometimes people pay for the mistakes we make; it's a weight you have to carry. You just … convince yourself it's getting lighter."

"How do you cope with it?" asked Elliot.

"Who says I'm coping?" replied Valentine, holding up a bottle of scotch, a pained smile on his face, his eyes shadowing regret. "Try not to linger on it like I have. You gave two kids a chance today. Try to remember that."

"I just wanna be alone for a bit," said Elliot.

Valentine nodded. "Yeah, all right. We're all here if you need us."

Valentine strolled through the city, going nowhere in particular. He wore a long black coat that closely resembled the robe he wore as a Reaper, the collar of the jacket pulled up around his neck.

Thick gray clouds were gathering overhead, and a light, cold drizzle began to fall.

Valentine reached into the small burgundy pouch that clung to his belt and produced a black umbrella. The rain grew heavier and heavier, and the air got colder, but Valentine didn't mind. The cold hadn't bothered him in a long time.

He came upon a box that was soaked with rain and had collapsed on itself. Something told him to look in the box. Valentine knelt down and rested the umbrella on the pavement. He opened the box and saw a puppy lying still. He put a hand on its neck; it was cold and lifeless. "Poor little thing," said Valentine in a sad voice. "Perhaps you could come home with me." Valentine concentrated his power and ran his hand over the lifeless puppy. Its fur began to turn from a light blond to pitch-black.

The dog softly kicked its legs and blinked to life. Looking up at Valentine, it let out a soft whimper.

"Come here, little one," said Valentine, picking up the puppy and pulling it to his chest. "You and I are not so different, now," he said to the dog. "I'm sorry you were left to die like that, little one. But I have a special job for you now."

The puppy reached up and licked his face.

Valentine tucked the puppy into a pocket inside his coat to shelter it. Adjusting his collar and picking up the umbrella, he headed back the way he came.

"How is he?" Valentine asked Rebecca.

"Hasn't come out of his room all day. Any idea what's bothering him?" she asked.

"He's got some stuff on his mind, nothing he can't work out," replied Valentine.

Valentine went to Elliot's room and knocked on the door. After not receiving an answer, he knocked again.

"Go away," Elliot called out.

"I'm coming in, I've got something you might like," said Valentine, opening the door.

"What do you want?" asked Elliot.

"Got something for you," replied Valentine. He reached into his coat, took the puppy out, and handed it to Elliot.

"Where did you get this?"

"Found him. Someone left him to die."

"Doesn't look quite like a normal puppy," said Elliot.

"It's a hellhound. I put some of the Reaper inside it."

"It's mine?" asked Elliot.

"Yeah, all yours. They get big though so be ready."

"Thanks," said Elliot, taking the puppy into his arms.

"Going after an arms dealer tonight. Wanna come?" asked Valentine.

"Y'know, I'm all set on the Reaper thing for now. I think I need a break for a bit."

"Well, just remember not to break for too long."

"Yeah, I know …" Elliot held the dog in his lap. Before Valentine closed the door, Elliot called out to him. "Hey, thanks."

"Don't mention it," replied Valentine, giving Elliot a subtle nod.

Valentine had heard a rumor from one of his dubious contacts that a weapons deal would be taking place somewhere in the old shipping yard on the west side. The area was crammed with large shipping containers, all stacked next to or on top of each other. Valentine was perched atop a crane, from which he had a view of the whole area. His cloak fluttered in the wind that rolled in from the sea. He had his hood pulled way down, completely obscuring his skull from the light of the moon. A passerby below would never notice him, seeing only the rich darkness of the sky.

He waited for most of the night and was starting to have second thoughts about the rumors when he spotted a van coming in from the south side of the yard and a car followed by a van entering from the east side. He shifted his position to center his view on the vehicles and watched them park. He was waiting for people to exit the vehicles before making his move.

Six men exited the first van, rifles in their hands but pointed at the ground.

Two men exited the car wearing tailored suits, and four men emerged from the van behind them, also carrying rifles at the ready.

Valentine moved in on the men silently, keeping to the darkness and watching from the shadows, listening in on the conversation.

After a few moments of talking, one of the men in a suit made a gesture with his hand, and the four armed men behind him moved with haste to their van and removed two small, square wooden crates and one long rectangular one.

One of the six armed men from the first van made a similar gesture with his hand, and one of the other men produced a briefcase from the vehicle and threw it over to the man in the suit.

The man opened the briefcase and observed its contents for a moment before closing it and waving his hand in a forward motion. His men carried the three crates to the other men and helped load them into the van.

Valentine was more concerned with the buyer than the seller, but if he could get them all, then it would be a good night's work for him. Moving in the shadows, he closed the distance between himself and the men. Focusing his power, he extended both his arms and pulled a storage container down. With a thunderous crash, it blocked one of the exits. He leaped from the shadows with his sword drawn and raised over his shoulder but was struck by a blinding mass of darkness.

Betraying his reclusiveness for hunger, Elliot left his room, his new puppy trailing behind him in a happy trot. Making his way into the kitchen, he put on a pot of coffee and put a bagel into the toaster. Having made his breakfast, he made his way outside to enjoy it on the patio. It was midmorning, and he hadn't seen Valentine yet. Usually he would've announced himself by then, a glass of scotch in hand.

Out in the yard, Warren was tending to the livestock.

"Hey, Warren!" Elliot called out, walking in Warren's direction.

"Good morning, Mister Blythe. How are you?" Warren answered.

"Just Elliot, please."

"Well, 'Just Elliot,' what can I do ya for?"

Elliot chuckled for Warren's benefit. "Hey, have you seen Valentine at all last night or this morning?" he asked.

"Hmm." Warren thought about it for a moment. "I don't believe I have. He prefers to slip in and out quietly. Perhaps you could ask Miss Rebecca. She seems to be rather fond of him," he suggested.

"Hmm, thanks," Elliot replied, trying not to sound too disappointed with the answer. He made his way back to the house and knocked on the door to Bex's room. "Fuck, that's right," he said to himself, remembering she had left earlier that morning for work. He took his phone out of his pocket and called her. "Hey, you see Valentine at all before you left?" he asked when Bex answered.

"No, I don't think so. Why?" she answered.

"Just wondering," Elliot replied. "I'll catch ya later." He hung up and called Valentine's phone, but it went straight to voice mail. "Hey, shoot me a text when you get this." Elliot put his phone away and then made his way back out to the patio. He took a sip of his coffee, but it had gone cold.

"Any luck?" asked Warren, walking up to the house.

"No, not yet," Elliot answered.

"Well, he'll turn up eventually. He's not one to stay out forever."

"Hey, uhm …" Elliot started. "How-how exactly did you find out that Valentine is uh … uhm …"

"A Reaper?" asked Warren, finishing the question.

Elliot nodded in reply.

"Known him a long time. I always knew he was a bit different, the way he raged through battles unscathed."

"So how did you find out?" Elliot asked, trying to keep Warren on track.

"Well, eventually he told me. Of course, I didn't believe him at the time. Wasn't until years later when I was peddlin' when I saw him. Hadn't aged a day. Really helped me get on my feet, he did."

Elliot nodded again. "So you and him met in the war?"

"Met in basic training, him and I," Warren replied. "He'll turn up eventually," he assured Elliot.

Night fell, and there was still no sign of Valentine anywhere. Rebecca had checked every room in the house when she returned from work, even calling him a couple of times. Elliot also left him another voice mail.

"I'm getting kinda worried," Rebecca confided to Elliot.

Elliot thought for a moment. "I'll find him," he told Rebecca before leaving the house. He made his way over to Warren's cabin on the edge of the property and knocked on the door.

Warren greeted him and invited him inside. "What brings ya by?" he asked, offering Elliot a beer.

"I'm all set," said Elliot, rejecting the beer. "Still no sign of Valentine."

"Hmm, rather peculiar, I'll admit," Warren replied, resting himself back in his worn recliner.

"Valentine knows a bounty hunter named Blue. Do you know her?"

Warren thought for a moment. "'Fraid I don't," he replied.

Elliot contemplated an idea. "You know anything about the Outer Darkness?" he asked.

"Now that, I think I can help you with," said Warren.

Warren led Elliot to Valentine's meditation room.

Elliot remembered the beautiful stone architecture.

"Has something to do with this spot right here," said Warren, pointing at a symbol etched into one of the stones in the floor.

Elliot recalled Valentine just making an elevator out of nothing. "Anything else?" he asked Warren.

"S'all I know."

"Hmm," Elliot hummed, letting out a heavy sigh. He extended his hands toward the symbol on the floor. Closing his eyes, he called on the power of the Reaper to help him.

A thick cloud of black smoke gathered in the center of the room in a large mass and then gave way to reveal the elevator that Elliot had been looking for.

Elliot stepped into the elevator.

"Don't get lost in there!" Warren called out as the elevator descended into darkness.

CHAPTER 11

MIDNIGHT BLUES

As Elliot continued to descend, the darkness that consumed him turned him into the Reaper. His skull was covered by his short black cloak. His boots echoed on the metal platform as he stepped off the elevator and crunched as he stepped onto the rocky depths of the Outer Darkness.

The familiar scenery of a fiery red sky with a menacing black castle loomed in the distance. Elliot tried to ignore the sounds of pained hellish screams, wailing somewhere in the distance.

Elliot made his way down a network of black roads, pushing his way through crowds of menacing-looking creatures and demons. He finally found the bar that Valentine had once brought him to. Stepping inside, he started scanning the room, hoping to find Blue. As he made his way to the counter, the large and grotesque creature known as Dante greeted him.

"Mmm, welcome back," said Dante in his growly voice.

"I'm looking for Blue. Seen her around?" Elliot asked.

"In her usual spot," replied Dante, pointing a hooked finger toward the back of the room.

As Elliot had hoped, she was sitting in the corner, playing a card game and gambling. Elliot pushed through the busy room and made his way over to the corner where Blue was seated.

"Hey, shadow boy," she said, her focus still on the game. "V let you off your leash?" she asked, looking up for a brief second and then returning her eyes to her cards.

"That's what I wanted to talk to you about," said Elliot, ignoring her comment. "He's missing."

Blue looked up at Elliot. Her face was straight, but there was a slight look of puzzlement in her gray eyes. She put her cards down on the table. "I'm out," she said, standing up from the table. "Follow me," she instructed Elliot. She led him across the room to the left side of the bar. After giving the bartender a wave, the two walked down a hall, and the bartender opened a secret room in the wall. Once they were inside, the door closed behind them. Blue took a seat on a cushioned bench next to a table and motioned for Elliot to sit across from her. "Now, what do you mean he's *missing?*" she asked, opening a bottle of black wine and pouring it into a glass.

"Haven't seen or heard from him since last night," Elliot replied.

"Not really like him to just go missing," Blue commented, taking a sip of her drink.

"So I've heard. I've tried calling, but he hasn't returned them," said Elliot.

"Yeah, been there," Blue remarked. "Did he say where he was going when you saw him last?" she inquired.

"Said he was investigating an arms deal," Elliot answered.

"He say where?"

Elliot shook his head. "Thoughts?" he asked.

Blue leaned back in her seat, kicked her boots up on the table, and ran a hand through her short blue hair. "He *does* have a lot of enemies," Blue noted.

"He hasn't mentioned anyone," said Elliot.

"Yeah, he tends to keep that sort of shit to himself."

"You can track him, can't you?" Elliot asked.

"That'll be two he owes me, getting his ass out of trouble. And one from you as well." Blue scoffed. "Yeah, I can track the bastard. You're gonna need more than just those ordinary swords if something is out there hunting Reapers."

"Suggestions?"

"Valentine went to someone down here in the darkness and had part of his Reaper forged into his sword. Could do that," she suggested.

"Know where he went?" Elliot asked.

"Yeah, I can take you there."

Blue led Elliot out into the streets and pushed through the crowd of creatures that inhabited them.

The Outer Darkness was far bigger than Elliot had realized. It was a whole other world. The streets were lined with various shops filled with weapons or curios. An outside market sold strange foods that Elliot had never seen before. Another shop had assorted severed body parts from a variety of creatures hanging from strings in the front.

They turned left down an alley and headed down into a tunnel that expanded into a massive underground dome with a lava lake down below. Keeping to the left, they entered a short cave with stalagmites that glowed red from the torches on the wall. At the end of the cave was a small metal door.

Blue knocked on the door. A small hatch in the door slid open, and a pair of yellow eyes peered out.

"Ah, Blue! Come in!" came a harsh, scratchy voice.

The door creaked open, and they were greeted by a small, red lizard-like creature that walked on its hind legs. A spiked tail dragged along on the ground behind it.

"How ya doin', Zida?" Blue chimed. "This is Elliot. He's a friend of Valentine's."

"How can I be of ssservicsse?" Zida hissed, a long tongue protruding from his fanged snout.

"We were wondering if you could help us forge blades like you did for Valentine," Blue answered.

"Ah, yesssss. It can be done. The bladesss you speak of are forged from the sssoulsss of the damned, here in the Outer Darknesssss," said Zida. "Lucky for you, I have sssome here."

Elliot watched Zida as he drew in a large breath and exhaled a white flame into a forge made from volcanic rock, fueled by toxic gases. He reached into a pool that looked like it was filled with oil and pulled out a horrid creature that let out an ear-splitting screech as it surfaced. The strange creature was nothing more than a skull and spinal cord. Pieces of rotten flesh clung to the bone, and black tentacles flailed frantically from its center. Zida took the creature and shoved it into the forge. It let out another screech as it melted in the flames.

"Presssent the bladesss you wish to usssse," hissed Zida.

Elliot drew his two swords and handed them over.

Zida took the swords and slid them into the forge. After a few moments, he removed the swords from the heat and dipped them into a red liquid. "Forged in Hellfire, binded by the ssoulsss of the damned, and bathed in the blood of ssinnersss," he said as the red liquid boiled and bubbled, sending an acrid iron odor into the air. "Your sswordsss," said Zida, holding them up to Elliot.

Elliot grabbed them. He could feel a powerful energy flowing through the swords, and the blade emanated an immense heat. "Thank you," he said to Zida.

"Of coursssssse."

Elliot brought Blue back to the farmhouse.

"Been a while since I've seen this place," Blue commented.

"Can you track him from here?" Elliot asked.

Blue looked around. She could see two thin black trails, one of which led to Elliot. "Yeah. I can see his footprint," she replied.

"I can't see anything," said Elliot.

"That's because you're not a *hunter*, shadow boy." She paced around the room. "So, I know you said he was going to an arms deal, but did he say *where*?"

Elliot shook his head. "Only mentioned the arms deal," he replied.

She tightened the cloth wrappings on her hands and wrists. "All right, let's go find his sorry ass."

"So, Valentine mentioned he was once one of your bounties," said Elliot, trying to spark a conversation with Blue as they walked silently through the city.

"And look where I am now, tracking him down again. At least some things never change," Blue replied.

Elliot could tell there was some personal tension between her and Valentine. "So what happened the first time?" he asked, inquiring further.

"I was chasing his ass. Had him cornered too. But the client hired someone else to take both of us out. For a while, we had each other's back."

"Did something happen between you two?"

"He hasn't told you?" asked Blue, sounding surprised.

Elliot shook his head.

"Huh. Well, we used to kinda see each other."

"What happened?"

"Just … two different people, I guess."

Blue tracked Valentine all the way to the harbor where he had gone for the arms deal. She moved her head around in all directions, observing Valentine's invisible footprint and looking for clues. "He went to the top of that crane," she said, pointing upward. "Then he came down. Let's go look over there."

Elliot followed her to the docks piled with shipping containers.

"Yeah, look, he came over behind this container here, and then he moved out into the open. But his trail goes cold right here," said Blue, indicating a spot on the pavement.

"There's tire tracks. At least two sets," Elliot pointed out. "What do you think happened?"

"Sshhh, I think I found something."

"What?" asked Elliot, moving to where Blue was.

"There's another Reaper print here," said Blue.

"Valentine?"

"No."

"What do you mean?" asked Elliot.

"I *mean* that it's not fucking Valentine. I can draw some sort of picture if you need me to." Blue took a deep breath. "Not like him to be blindsided like that," she muttered to herself.

"Should we follow it?" Elliot suggested.

Blue nodded but didn't say anything. She feared that something may have happened to Valentine but didn't want her emotion to show in the tone of her voice. "Let's go," she forced out.

CHAPTER 12

TO CATCH A REAPER

The new trail that Blue and Elliot were following led them all the way to the mills on the west side of the city.

"I've been here with Valentine," Elliot chirped.

They followed the trail through the building that Elliot had accidentally blown up.

"The trail goes everywhere from here," said Blue.

"Well, pick a direction, and I'll follow."

"That's the problem; the trail seems to go in circles around here and spirals off in different directions." She moved around the burned building, kicking ash and chunks of wood around as she walked. She walked to the same corner that Elliot had been in when the building exploded. She kicked the ash away to reveal a wooden panel in the floor. "Hey, check this out," she called to Elliot.

"What's up?" he asked, joining Blue at her side.

Blue lifted up the wooden panel to find a large metal door in the concrete foundation. "Trail leads into here."

Elliot concluded that if the building hadn't exploded when he entered this area, he would have found the hidden door. Lost in thought, he hadn't noticed that Blue had opened the door and made her way inside. "Hey, wait up!" he called after her.

Beneath the old mill was a labyrinth of pristine white halls and rooms that had been converted into small labs. People in masks and white suits worked diligently on their tasks inside the labs, some attending computer screens, some swirling beakers, and others carrying containers and various tools and equipment. None paid any attention to Blue and Elliot.

The two began walking down the hall, looking for anything that might indicate where they were going.

"I had no idea there was a whole lab under Sterling City," said Elliot.

"Something tells me Valentine didn't either," replied Blue.

"Valentine and I didn't see this on the power grid."

"It's probably on its own," replied Blue. "Keep a low profile. We don't want anyone knowing we're here."

"Yes, m'lord," Elliot teased.

Blue turned and glared at Elliot, and then she continued walking.

A scientist in a white suit stepped out of a lab and almost bumped right into Blue. He turned to call out to his peers, but before he could, Elliot extended one of his arms and using the Reaper's powers, pulled the scientist quickly toward him. He was stopped by the sword that Elliot thrust through his sternum, his flesh sizzling from the heat of the blade. The man leaned over Elliot's shoulder and made a gurgling noise.

Elliot opened a hole to the darkness and tossed the man into it. "Keep a low profile," he said to Blue.

Blue tilted her head slightly. "I'll kick your ass, shadow boy." She walked further down the hall. "It splits up here in two directions, and there's an elevator right there."

"Would really help if we knew where the fuck we were going," said Elliot. Just then, he had a thought. "I have an idea. It's a little fucked up, but bear with me," he said. Walking over to a lab door, he knocked on it and then ducked from view.

"What are you doing?" asked Blue, her eyes wide.

"Trust me," Elliot assured her.

A scientist came to the door and opened it, peering out into the hall to see who knocked.

Elliot sprang out from around the corner. Grabbing the man by his face, Elliot pulled him from the doorway and out of view of the labs. Pinning the man to the ground, Elliot used his powers to invade the man's mind and read his thoughts and memories. Elliot removed his hand from the man's head to let him up, but the Reaper's power had left him brain dead.

"Jesus Christ, you fried the motherfucker. Did you at least figure anything out?" asked Blue.

"Live subjects are being held on the bottom level."

Blue got into the elevator. "We need his hand," she called out, pointing at a biometric scanner.

Elliot unsheathed his sword and removed the man's hand before tossing him into the darkness. He walked over to the scanner and placed the severed hand on it.

Blue face-palmed herself. "Not exactly what I had in mind when I said that," she remarked.

The elevator dinged, and the doors opened.

"Hey, it worked, didn't it?" replied Elliot. "I know you can't see it, but I'm grinning."

"You Reapers are all the same," said Blue, pushing the button labeled "C."

The bottom level split off into three directions: crematorium, holding, and testing.

Elliot stood still, a cold sensation running down his spine. Reaching out into the expanse of the building with the Reaper's powers, he could almost hear Valentine's voice. "He's here," he said to Blue.

"Not in the crematorium, I hope."

They both moved at a fast pace to the holding area of the floor. Dozens of people were locked in cages. Some were strapped down to tables; all of them were emaciated. Some even had limbs that had been poorly removed. Though bandaged, they were still bleeding. Pained moans echoed off the walls.

Elliot slowly made his way across the room, looking into the cages for any sign of Valentine.

Some of the prisoners pressed up against their confines and reached out toward Elliot, trying to grasp at his robe as he walked by. "Kill me!" one of them called out.

"Please, please, kill me!" sobbed another.

"Take me!" cried others.

Elliot pitied them, but he needed to find Valentine first.

A female scientist walked into the room and gasped at the sight of Elliot.

Elliot whirled on her and was about to make a move when she stuck up her hands.

"Please don't kill me!" she begged.

Elliot took a step back and gave her some space.

"Y-you must be looking for the one they brought in. He looked like you," the woman said, gesturing to Elliot's robes. "I can show you where he is."

"Why would you do that?" Elliot asked in a distrusting tone.

"The man in charge," she started. "He holds us prisoner here. If I help you, will you help me?"

"Let's focus on the first part for now," replied Elliot.

Just then, an alarm sounded, and the doors to the holding wing closed and locked themselves. Gas began pouring out from vents high on the walls. Prisoners screamed and yelled as they clawed at their throats.

Elliot's vision started to get hazy.

"We need to get out of here!" the woman yelled. "Quick, come with me."

Blue grabbed the handles of the doors and yanked on them, but they wouldn't budge. She took a few steps back and braced her feet on the floor. She drew in a deep breath, moving her hands up her torso as she inhaled. Stepping forward and extending her hands quickly, she expelled a blinding ball of blue flame that smashed into the door, knocking it off its hinges.

"Let's go!" The scientist beckoned. "They're coming!"

Elliot and Blue took off down the hall. As they turned left toward the testing area, armed guards began running after them from behind.

"Go!" Blue yelled to Elliot. She stopped in the hall and turned to face the mercenaries. Taking another deep breath, she exhaled a long blue flame that swirled down the hall, engulfing all of the men and burning them.

Elliot could hear their screams from the other side of the hall.

Blue took off after Elliot.

Inside the testing area were several tables with dissected bodies lying on them. Vats of green liquid stretched to the ceiling and were connected via pipes that ran between them. Elliot saw a glass gas chamber, similar to the one he had been in on the prison ship.

"Elliot!" Blue called out.

Elliot turned and saw Blue standing in a doorway, holding the door open, a pained look on her face and a tear swelling in her eye. Elliot quickly rushed over and saw Valentine suspended in an arch with glowing restraints on his hands and feet.

Valentine looked weak, and his skin was pale. His head hung down, and he was unresponsive when Elliot approached him.

Blue found the control modules and hit a button that cut the power to the machine, releasing Valentine.

Elliot quickly moved in and caught him before he hit the ground.

Blue rushed to his side and pushed the hair out of his face. Putting her cheek over his mouth and her fingers on his neck, she waited. "He's still alive!" she exclaimed, almost bursting into tears.

"The doctor has used an experimental nerve agent on him," said the woman.

A clapping echoed throughout the room.

Elliot turned and saw Meier standing in the doorway.

"How touching, almost brings a tear to my eye," he jested, a twisted grin on his face. "I'll admit, I was rather surprised to see that you had survived the explosion." He tilted his nose up in a sort of arrogant disgust. "I was wondering when we would meet again. After the botched assassination, I figured it was only a matter of time. It appears you're a hard one to kill."

Elliot drew his swords and was ready to make a move on Meier.

"I wouldn't if I were you." Meier stepped aside as a large man with long silver hair entered the room.

"Novak," Elliot muttered.

"Hello, old China. Miss me?"

"It's a shame you weren't in time to save him," Meier antagonized. "And you, Doctor," he said, addressing the woman, "I'm afraid we'll have to terminate your employment." He turned his head slightly to Novak. "Kill them."

Before Meier could retreat out the door, Blue expelled a burst of fire in his direction.

Meier dove out of the way as the fire struck a pipe, causing it to burst and spray a green liquid everywhere.

Meier screamed in pain as the liquid splashed onto the right side of his face, melting the skin. Removing a glass vial from his belt, he threw it at Elliot's feet and escaped down the hallway, a dozen or more mercenaries running in the opposite direction as he and entering the room.

Blue braced her feet and sent a plume of fire spinning ferociously down the hallway, engulfing the mercenaries who were entering the room and setting them ablaze.

The vial broke, and the chemical inside caused Elliot's brain and vision to spin. An intense pain buried itself deep inside him and spread throughout his body.

More mercenaries made their way down the hallway, stepping over the burned corpses of their comrades.

"Take Valentine, and get out of here!" Blue barked. She moved her arms in a whipping motion, and fire spiraled around the room, creating a ring around them.

Novak jumped backward and grunted as the flames flashed in his face, but he deflected them and avoided injury. Regaining his focus, he sprang toward Blue, a large knife clutched in his hand.

Elliot grabbed Valentine and opened a path into the darkness. He dived into it while dragging Valentine behind him. Before the opening could close, Elliot shot a burst of black energy at Novak, hitting him in the chest and knocking him backward. Reaching out with his powers, he pulled Blue into the darkness.

The darkness turned to light, and the three of them crashed onto the wooden floor of Misha's cabin in the forest.

Misha emerged in a hurry from a room divided by a purple curtain.

"Misha! Y-you have to help Val—" Elliot tried to say before reverting to his human form and falling unconscious.

"Misha, it's Blue," said Blue, putting a hand on Misha's shoulder and guiding her over to Elliot and Valentine. "We found Valentine in a lab. We don't know what's wrong with him, and Elliot has been exposed to some sort of nerve gas."

Misha knelt down on the floor and placed her hands on Valentine's chest. She shuffled over and placed her hands on Elliot. "Hmm."

"What is it?" Blue asked.

"It appears that whatever they were exposed to is diminishing the connection to their Reapers, sending it into a sort of paralysis," Misha replied.

"Can you help them?" Blue asked in urgency.

"I believe so," Misha replied. She stood up and began rummaging through the drawers and shelves, tossing random objects to her left and right until she found what she wanted. She set out an assortment of bottles and vials filled with powders and coagulated liquids. "Can you get them onto the beds in the other room while I prepare things?"

Blue nodded and then remembered Misha couldn't see her. "Yes," she said, picking up Valentine as gently as she could.

"Why don't you go make some tea for us? This will take some time," Misha said caringly.

"I don't wanna leave them," Blue replied.

"Go!" Misha ordered. After Blue left the room, Misha got to work. She started by drawing a strange symbol in black on Valentine and Elliot. Lighting candles, she clasped her hands together, bowed her head, and muttered a prayer in a strange language over each of them. She set fire to a bushel of herbs and waved it in the air, cascading Elliot and Valentine with smoke. She poured a thick black liquid into a cup and poured it into their mouths. She drew a knife and grasped the blade in her free hand before sliding the knife in a downward position until it drew blood from her palm. Reciting another ancient prayer, she squeezed her hand and let the blood drip onto the symbols she had drawn on their chests. The blood boiled and bubbled on the symbol, and their chests raised as each took a breath.

Hours had passed before Elliot regained consciousness. He winced at the light that hung overhead. Looking over to his left, he saw Blue sitting on the edge of Valentine's bed, running a hand through his hair. He groaned as he tried to sit upright in his bed, but moving made it seem like the whole room was spinning.

Blue, realizing Elliot was awake, got him a glass of the black liquid Misha had made. "Here, drink this," she said, handing the cup to Elliot.

He took a sip and gagged. "This tastes how dirty shoes smell."

"Misha's orders," Blue replied. "How ya feelin'?"

Elliot sighed as he rubbed his eyes. "I feel like I've been hit by a truck," he replied. He looked around the room. "Where's that woman that was with us?"

"I'm not sure," Blue replied. "Listen, uh, thanks for saving my ass back there."

Just then, Valentine rolled over and vomited on the floor. He let out a pained groan. Propping himself up on his right arm, he looked around, taking in his surroundings and realizing where he was.

Blue moved to his side, sat on the edge of the bed, and told him to rest.

"What happened?" asked Valentine in a daze.

"Meier was holding you prisoner. He drugged you with some kind of nerve agent," Blue replied.

Valentine nodded and then put his head back on the pillow. "They had the drop on me. I think they thought I was you," he said, turning to Elliot.

"I thought you said nothing could harm a Reaper," said Elliot.

"Guess I was wrong," said Valentine. "Meier has a plan to destroy the city," he said, sounding somewhat defeated. "Those tanks were filled with a milder form of his chemical." Valentine tried to stand up but fell to his knees. "I can't fight like this," he said.

Blue helped him back onto the bed.

"It's only a matter of time before he infects the whole city." Elliot sighed heavily.

"Just rest for now. We'll figure it out," said Blue, leaving the room.

CHAPTER 13

THE GRAND PLAN

"You never mentioned Novak was a Reaper," said Valentine, sitting on the edge of the bed, rubbing his face.

"I didn't know," Elliot replied, sitting up. "What happened?" he asked.

Valentine sighed as he tried to recollect the events of the past few hours. "I remember moving in on the deal. I think that's when Novak ambushed me. Next thing I knew, I was in some sort of lab."

"We got you out of there just in time," said Elliot.

"Yeah, thanks for that."

Misha came into the room, holding a kettle in one hand and two wooden cups in the other. "Good to hear that you boys are awake," she said. She handed a cup to Valentine and poured a steaming red liquid in it; then she repeated the process with Elliot and ordered them both to drink all of it.

"What is it?" Elliot asked, observing the liquid as he swirled it in the cup.

"Drink!" Misha ordered and left the room.

"Seriously though, what is this?" asked Elliot, turning to Valentine.

Valentine lifted the cup to his face and sniffed it before taking a sip. His face twisted from the bitter taste. "I think it's demon's blood," he said, forcing down another sip.

Elliot curled his nose and groaned before knocking it all back. He almost threw it up on the floor but managed to keep it down. "That's just fucking awful," he choked out.

Valentine finished his cup without a fuss. He looked at his hands and focused on them. Black smoke rolled over his fingertips as his hands turned to bone. "Feeling better at least," he said. "So, what's the plan?"

Elliot shook his head in silence. "Thoughts?" he asked.

"I think we best head back to the lab," Valentine replied. "Feeling up for it?"

Elliot nodded. "Ready when you are."

When Elliot, Valentine, and Blue got back to the abandoned mills on the west side, groups of mercenaries were outside patrolling the area. The trio sneaked into an empty building and observed the mercenary movements through a dusty window.

"What do you think's going on?" asked Blue.

"It looks like they're preparing for something. We need to move in and figure out what they're up to," said Valentine. "Still have your earpiece?" he asked Elliot.

Elliot responded with a single nod.

"Here, take this," he said, handing one to Blue. "All right, let's go. Keep to the shadows."

"I'll stay here and keep watch on everything else," said Blue.

"Not a bad idea," said Valentine. "Tell us if you see anything."

Elliot followed Valentine out into the streets. Keeping to the shadows, they crossed over to an adjacent building.

"Two coming your way," said Blue.

Valentine nodded to Elliot, who nodded back.

As the two guards walked in front of the shadow, long black tentacles shot out and wrapped around their mouths and torsos and pulled them into the darkness where they vanished.

"Nice," Blue remarked in the earpiece.

Valentine and Elliot crept onward, avoiding the guards to the best of their ability. As they approached the building with the hidden door to the lab, they saw the orange glow of fire. They moved closer to get a view and saw fire shooting from the entrance to the lab. Guards stood around the flames, joking and laughing.

"What do you think is going on?" Elliot asked Valentine.

113

"Destroying evidence," Valentine replied. "They've moved everything. They must have been anticipating us."

Just then, Blue called through the earpiece. "I'm on a truck!"

"*What?*" asked Valentine.

"They were moving something in a truck. I climbed into the back," Blue replied.

"That wasn't the plan," said Valentine, exasperated.

"Too late!" Blue called back.

"You sure it was a good idea bringing her along?" Elliot asked Valentine.

"She *insisted*."

"I can still hear you, you fuckin' boneheads," said Blue through the earpiece.

"Whoops," said Elliot. "What do we do about the guards here?" he asked.

"We shouldn't leave them," replied Valentine. "Make sure they don't raise any alarms or reach for a radio."

"Aye, aye, sir!" said Elliot, giving a salute. He crept up silently on an unsuspecting guard. Drawing a sword with his right hand, he wrapped his left arm around the guard's head and pulled him backward as he impaled his chest.

Valentine glided over to the group of men standing around the fire. He drew his sword, and with a swift motion, he beheaded two of the guards. He extended his left arm and expelled a black mass of energy from his hand that struck the third guard, knocking him down into the lab, which was now a blazing inferno. From his peripheral, Valentine spotted a fourth guard over to his right. Reaching out with his powers, he grabbed the man and yanked him forward as Valentine thrust his sword into his chest.

"Hey, Valentine!" Elliot called out, moving quickly over to Valentine. "One of the men had a detonator on him," Elliot extended his hand to show Valentine the small device.

"Fuck." Valentine took a deep breath. "It must be connected to one of the warheads they stole."

"Well, it's gotta be nearby then. What's near here?"

"Downtown West is only a mile from here."

"Hey, guys," Blue said through the earpiece, a sense of urgency in her voice. "Got a bit of a situation here."

"What's going on, Blue?" asked Valentine, matching her level of urgency.

"This truck's got a bomb on it."

"Fuck. Where are you?"

"Looks like … Downtown East."

Valentine's phone vibrated, and he drew it from his robe. It was a text from the commissioner. "Meet me ASAP."

Valentine walked over to one of the dead mercenaries and took the handheld radio from his utility vest.

Commissioner Lowell paced frantically back and forth on the roof of the precinct, taking rapid drags from his cigarette. He turned around and saw that Valentine and Elliot had silently appeared behind him, silhouetted against the light of the moon. He took one last drag from his cigarette before tossing it down and twisting his foot on it. "There are *two* of you now?" he asked.

"Your text seemed urgent. I brought backup. Get to the point, Commissioner."

"The city hall has been overrun," said the commissioner. He reached into his jacket and pulled out another cigarette. His hand shook as he lit it. "A bunch of mercenaries have taken the mayor and some of the staff hostage."

"Have they made demands?" Valentine asked.

"Only that no one enters the building, or they'll start killing hostages," Lowell replied.

Valentine turned his head slightly in Elliot's direction. "You think it's Meier?" he asked in a low voice.

"Has to be."

"Have your men formed a perimeter around the building, Commissioner?" asked Valentine, turning back to Lowell.

"Yes, all the way around. No one is getting in or out." Lowell had already finished his cigarette and was lighting a third.

"Have them hold their positions. *We* will get in there," Valentine ordered in a stern tone.

Elliot and Valentine manifested themselves outside the city hall. What seemed like every police officer in Sterling City had gathered to form a perimeter around the building. Red and blue lights danced in circles against the exterior of the building. Some of the officers were holding their positions facing the city hall while others worked to keep a growing crowd of bystanders away from the area. Three officers carrying an injured comrade were retreating from the building after a failed entry attempt.

Commissioner Lowell pulled up in his car in time to see the wounded officer be put into an ambulance. Furious, he stormed toward the officer in charge. "I said *no* attempts at entry!" he screamed at the man. When he was finished scolding the officer, he approached Elliot and Valentine. "I don't want a *single* hostage harmed," he growled.

"Don't tell me how to do my job. I've seen the results of how your men do *theirs*," Valentine snapped back.

Lowell clenched his fists and gritted his teeth but said nothing. He turned his back and walked over to the ambulance to check on the wounded officer.

Valentine moved to the officer in charge.

The officer, intimidated and startled by the two Reapers, jumped backward.

"What do you know about the situation?" Valentine asked.

"A-at least a dozen staff being held hostage, plus the mayor. Between forty and fifty armed suspects," the officer replied.

"Do you know what floor the mayor is on?"

"No."

"Right then, let's get on with it," Valentine said to Elliot.

A voice came over the radio that Valentine had taken. "Third and final bomb in place."

"Good," came a reply. Elliot recognized the voice as Meier's.

"There's been no reply from Alpha group. I think they may have been compromised," said the first voice.

CHAPTER 14

THE STANDOFF

Blue rode in the back of the covered truck, trying to keep as silent as possible until they stopped.

The truck finally squealed to a halt, and five men got out.

Blue listened to them as they got closer to the back of the truck. As one of the mercenaries pulled the gate of the truck down, Blue leaped from cover, knocking the man down and landing on top of him. She extended her fist and expelled a burst of blue flames into the man's face.

The other four men quickly raised their rifles and pointed them at Blue.

Blue ducked down and kicked one of her legs out. She released a string of flame that whipped around and tripped the men, causing them to fall over. She expelled a massive wave of fire from her palms that scorched three of the men.

The fourth man rolled to the side and avoided the flames. He grabbed his rifle and regained his posture, but he wasn't quick enough.

Blue ran at him and delivered a powerful kick to his groin, causing the man to keel over in pain. She ripped the rifle from his hands and hit him over the head with it. When the man was on the ground, rolling in pain, Blue gifted the man with mercy in the form of a flame that consumed him.

She climbed back into the truck and pulled a blanket off the large object that had been in the back. "Hey, guys, got a bit of a situation here," she said into the earpiece. "This truck's got a bomb on it."

Valentine had asked her to see if she could try to disarm it.

After pulling off the front panel, she could see a tank filled with a green liquid. A mess of wires blanketed the tank and ran to a primer and explosive housing. "Fuck," she said to herself. She noticed there was no timing mechanism. "Val, these bombs are set for manual detonation," she said.

A bullet whizzed past Blue's head and ricocheted around the metal interior of the truck.

Turning in the direction of the shot, Blue saw a group of mercenaries who had heard the screams of their comrades. Leaping from the truck, she released a frenzy of fiery blasts from her fists. The mercenaries dove for cover from the flames.

Blue whipped a rope of flames around one man's neck, and he screamed in agony as it burned through his flesh. Yanking the flame with a whipping motion, she severed the man's head. She released a burst of flames at two men who had betrayed their cover and were greeted with a fiery end. Blue approached the last man, who stood his ground with his rifle raised. Blue grabbed the barrel of the rifle until it glowed red, and she bent the barrel backward, rendering the gun useless.

"I don't like hitting girls," the man growled, drawing a knife from his vest.

"I have no problem with it," replied Blue, delivering a fiery punch that went all the way through the man's head.

Elliot and Valentine entered the main foyer of city hall. A large crystal chandelier hung from the ceiling, and the walls were adorned with paintings of every Sterling City mayor. A red carpet stretched from the door and up a set of marble stairs. As the duo ascended the stairs, they were met by a group of mercenaries who had been alerted to their presence.

Drawing his sword, Valentine sliced the first man in half at the stomach.

Elliot leaped up the stairs and attacked the men from the rear, beheading one man and leaving a long, searing cut on the back of another. He grabbed the last man and tossed him over the edge of the stairs.

Blue's voice chimed through the earpiece. "Val, I've disabled the bomb. This whole thing is filled with that chemical we saw at the lab."

"Excellent work, Blue," Valentine congratulated her. "We think there's another bomb in Downtown West. See if you can make it there and disarm it."

"Copy that," replied Blue.

"We're at the city hall. There's word of a third bomb, but we think it's here, along with Meier."

"Be careful," urged Blue.

Elliot and Valentine navigated the hallways with their swords drawn.

Meier's voice came over the intercom. "Your insolent persistence to push forward is really growing on my nerves. Can you not see what I am trying to accomplish?" His voice echoed through the halls. "Humans are a disease, a *parasite*. We as a species destroy everything we touch, constantly soiling our progress toward the future, all the while destroying the earth. If I can cull the herd, the survivors can be guided and led to a better future."

"You're fucked up, Meier!" Elliot called out.

"You may not agree with my methods, but I'm sure even *you* agree there is wickedness on this earth."

"The only wicked one is you!" Elliot yelled back.

"Not from my perspective. From my point of view, everyone is sick, greedy, and inane. An execrable, feckless, and petulant species. Humans are a disease, and I am the healer!" Meier exclaimed. "Oh, and may I add, my *men* had three devices, excluding the one here. Your little friend won't be able to reach them all, and as a precaution, I have a little surprise for her—one I shall share with you as well."

As Meier finished speaking, large double doors burst open as three large men entered through the doorway. Each of the men were wearing hazmat suits and gas masks. They also carried large guns with hoses attached that ran to cylindrical tanks on their backs filled with a green liquid.

"Kill them!" Meier yelled over the intercom.

Elliot dove for cover as the men started expelling green gas in his direction. "Blue! Are you there?" he called.

"Yeah, I'm here." Her voice was barely audible over the sound of gunshots. "What's up?"

"There's more than three bombs!" Elliot replied.

"Well, I'll see what I can do." She grunted as the sound of gunshots grew louder. "Fuck, who are they?" Blue said to herself.

"Who are *who*?" asked Elliot.

"There's guys carrying chemical tanks on their backs."

The second bomb had been placed inside of a church.

Blue dove between the pews, dodging the volley of gunfire that followed her. She rolled from cover and hit two men square in the chest with fire blasts.

A group of mercenaries dove behind the cover of pews.

Summoning a large mass of fire, Blue sent it rolling over the pews like a massive wave that consumed everything in its path.

The church sanctuary echoed with the screams of the men as they burned.

Blue turned to the entrance to face the sound of a massive crash.

A group of men in suits and masks, carrying chemical tanks entered the sanctuary.

Blue pulled a cover from her neck up over her nose as an opaque green cloud began rolling its way toward her. Leaping from her position, she grabbed onto a chandelier and swung up to the choir balcony.

The men wielding the chemical tanks pushed forward as more mercenaries entered the church, protected by gas masks.

The church began to fill with the green smoke, and it was almost up to the balcony.

Blue had a sudden idea; it was risky, but it was the only way. She summoned a ball of flames in her palm and threw it toward the center of the cloud. The ball of flame splashed onto the ground and lit the cloud of gas on fire. The fire burned all the way through the cloud and up through the hoses to the chemical tanks, causing a massive explosion that sent waves rolling furiously in all directions, consuming all of the mercenaries in the sanctuary.

Blue charged through the flames to where the bomb was.

The intense heat of the fire in the building was causing the chemical inside the tank to boil, and the glass of the tank itself was starting to crack.

"Fuck!" said Blue. She created a massive dome of flames and covered the bomb with it.

The intense heat caused the tank to burst, but the chemical was quickly burned away by Blue's protective dome.

The force of the blast, however, was so strong that it sent Blue flying backward into the burning sanctuary. She smacked the back of her head on the stone floor, knocking her unconscious.

Valentine was expelling black masses of energy trying to stave off the cloud of green toxin. He slowly stepped backward, retreating as the cloud crept forward.

A plume of the toxin rolled in his direction but was diverted by a mass of energy from Elliot. "What are we gonna do?" he yelled to Valentine.

"Hold them off!" Valentine called back.

Elliot jumped to the center of the hall and took Valentine's place, battling the green cloud.

Valentine stepped backward and centered himself, focusing his energy. With a quick extension of his arms, he expelled a wave of energy that cut the power to every light in the hallway, consuming everyone in pitch-darkness.

Elliot winced as bloodcurdling screams echoed throughout the hall. When the lights flickered on again, Elliot could see streaks and pools of blood all over the floor and walls. The bodies of the mercenaries had been torn and shredded to pieces as if they had been attacked by some sort of feral beast. Elliot turned to Valentine.

"You all right, kid?" Valentine asked.

"Yeah, think so," Elliot replied.

"Blue, you there?" Valentine called out, but there was no reply. "Blue!" Still no reply. "I can't get word from Blue," he said to Elliot.

"Think something might have happened to her?" Elliot asked.

"There's no time to dwell on it. This thing ain't over. You go find Meier, and I'll locate the bomb and hostages." Valentine ordered. His cape twirled in the air as he turned to head through the double doors. He stopped and cocked his head over his shoulder. "Be careful, kid."

As Valentine made his way through city hall, he eventually came upon a set of large mahogany doors with brass handles. Pushing the doors opened, he entered the main chamber of the building. Past rows of seats, on the main stage, a bomb had been placed where the podium would normally sit. The city staff were all gagged and bound to the explosive device, with the exception of the mayor, who was nowhere to be seen. As Valentine moved forward into the room, he could see the desperate looks of pleading in their eyes.

Guarding the hostages, fifty of Novak's men stood ready to engage Valentine.

Fools, Valentine thought to himself. He snarled like a beast, leaping and twisting through the air. In a blinding motion, he sliced one man in half at the waist and then decapitated two more. Gliding forward in a blur, he sliced one man across the stomach, leaving him screaming in agony as he tried to keep his entrails from falling out. Spinning toward another man, he swung violently and sliced him in half from the groin upward. As the men started to close in on him, Valentine sheathed his sword and centered himself, clenching his fists and focusing his energy. He extended his arms in a quick motion. A black ring of energy rolled through the room with Valentine at its epicenter. The ring washed over the mercenaries, leaving a mass of dead bodies in its wake. The room fell silent.

The doors slammed behind Valentine, and a voice called out to him, "Come to get your ass kicked *again*? I'll put you in the grave where you belong." It was Novak, standing in the doorway, a short, black-bladed sword in each hand.

"You blindsided me," Valentine scoffed. "It *won't* happen again." He widened his stance and drew his sword.

Wasting no time, Novak rushed in on Valentine's position and waved his swords furiously.

"Oh, no foreplay?" Valentine asked, meeting Novak's swords with his own. "All right, snake, let's *rattle*." Valentine delivered a strong kick to Novak's chest, knocking him back a step.

Novak rushed in again with reckless abandon, swinging his swords inward in a scissor motion.

Valentine leaned back, the blades narrowly missing his skull.

Novak picked up the pace with his attacks, swinging violently left and right.

Valentine stepped back, dodging all of the blows, almost as if to mock Novak. "For some reason, I thought you'd be *better* than Elliot," he said sarcastically, continuing to dance away from the blades.

Novak roared with anger. "Fight me, you little fairy!" he yelled. He moved forward and plunged his swords downward in a failed attempt to impale Valentine.

Gliding silently to the side, Valentine moved behind Novak and swung his sword upward, leaving a searing gash on Novak's back.

Novak spun around and expelled a mass of energy at Valentine, but Valentine channeled the energy and directed it back at Novak, sending him flying backward and crashing into some seats. Picking himself up, he hurled a sword at Valentine.

Valentine waited for the precise moment and snatched the sword out of the air. Spinning around, he sent it back at Novak, impaling him in the shoulder. "Wounded by your own blade. *Sloppy*," he remarked.

Novak ripped the blade from his shoulder and let the power of his Reaper wash over him. His flesh melted from the bone as a black smoke washed over him. Instead of a cloak, he wore a black tunic that wrapped tightly around his bone. He let out a deafening scream.

Elliot wandered the halls of the building, looking for Meier. The lights in the building seemed to flicker with each step he took.

Meier spoke over the intercom. "I'll save us both some time," he said in an exasperated tone. "I'm in the mayoral office. Don't keep *us* waiting."

When Elliot reached the office, he found Meier sitting on the desk with his back turned to the door. His attention was fixed on the crowd of police officers that had gathered around the building. "Kind of funny, don't you think?" he said, still looking out the window. "I am your creator, yet here you are, set on killing me."

Elliot drew his swords. "You're nothing but a madman," he replied.

"I gave you your powers!" Meier turned toward Elliot, his scarred face concealed by a mask that almost resembled that of a plague doctor. "I know you've seen what a horrid species we can be."

"You're a prime example," Elliot fired back.

"Are you really any better than *me?*" Meier scoffed. "I aim to heal humanity. Think of the people you've killed."

"I wasn't killing innocents."

"Everyone is guilty of something. We're all selfish and out for our own gain. It's not so much killing as it is *culling.* Think of it like a controlled burn. Destroying the weak and useless to make way for the strong and powerful. The chosen few who will lead us to a greater future."

"Your plan won't work, Meier. We've already disabled three of your bombs."

"You really think that will be enough to stop me? Not only do I have overrides to the devices, but there are several more in development as we speak." Meier pushed himself off the desk and walked around to the large office chair that was turned away from Elliot's view. "There are things in motion that can't be undone. And try as you may, you are powerless to stop them." Meier turned the chair around so that Elliot could see the mayor, gagged and bound. A look of horror beamed in the man's eyes. "You and I …" Meier said in an ominous tone, "are simply pawns in a much larger game."

Before Elliot could ask what Meier had meant, there was a loud bang, and blood poured from the mayor's head.

"No!" Elliot yelled.

Elliot started to move in on Meier, but Meier reacted quickly and tossed a vial that erupted with a green smoke. Dazed by the toxin, Elliot used his powers to clear the room of the smoke, but by that time, Meier had escaped. Elliot rushed out into the hallway to chase after Meier. "Valentine, Meier has override activations for the bombs. You won't be able to disable them." Elliot could hear Valentine grunt on the other end of the transceiver.

"A little preoccupied at the moment," Valentine managed to say.

Valentine successfully parried several ferocious attacks from Novak. Stepping to his right, he raised his sword to parry a downward strike and then flipped his blade to deflect an upward swing. Seeing an opportunity, he stepped inward and raised his sword swiftly, severing Novak's left hand as the blade clanged on the floor.

Novak, enraged, leaped backward and expelled a massive burst of energy at Valentine, who had summoned his own.

The two masses of energy collided with each other and sent Valentine and Novak sailing backward through the air.

Novak jumped to his feet and let out another deafening screech as he raised his remaining hand.

Gargled moans and hisses filled the room. With slow, jerking motions, the mercenaries that Valentine had killed began picking themselves up from the ground. Their wounds were still fresh and their eyes devoid of life.

Valentine picked himself up and observed the situation. Grabbing his sword, he began hacking his way through the crowd of dead soldiers just as he had done before, only this time, he removed every head in his path to Novak. Sweeping his sword from left to right, he sent body parts flying through the air.

Novak raised his remaining hand toward Valentine to fend him off with a burst of energy, but before it could leave his fingertips, Valentine swung his sword and cut it off.

Valentine's face was covered in the blood of Novak's men. He extended his left arm, picking Novak up with an unseen hand.

Novak moved his mouth as if to speak, but the words were unable to escape.

"Tell me," said Valentine. "Do you feel dead?" He swung his sword and decapitated Novak.

Valentine let the body crumple to the floor as it turned to ash and vanished. He picked up Novak's bare skull and put it into the pouch that hung from his belt. He turned his attention to the hostages tied to the bomb. With a snap of his fingers, their bindings and gags vanished. Valentine waved a hand at them, stripping their memories of everything they had just seen. "Go. You're all safe now," he ordered them. He summoned a portal of darkness, and using his powers, he tossed the bomb into the opening and closed it.

Meier cackled maniacally, running down the hallway and tossing vials of chemicals over his shoulder as Elliot chased after him.

Elliot was using his powers to throw things at Meier and knock things over to obstruct his path, but it was to no avail.

Meier tossed another vial over his shoulder that erupted into a wall of flames, covering the width of the hallway.

Elliot walked through the flames without injury. A sword in his right hand, he used his left to snatch Meier with his powers.

Meier choked as he tried to speak. "You can defeat me, but where will it get you? I've already won. You've failed!" Before he was in reach of Elliot's sword, he drew another vial from his belt and threw it at Elliot, allowing for his escape and a continued pursuit. He opened a door and climbed a stairwell that led up to the roof. He had almost made it to the other side by the time Elliot recovered and made his way up.

Valentine appeared outside the church on the west side. The building had been reduced to a heaping pile of smoldering rubble. Only a few charred pieces of the frame still stood. He moved silently across the hot embers, his cloak and the smoke of the fire flowing together almost as if they were one. Reaching out with his senses, he could feel Blue nearby. Removing pieces of rubble and charred wood, he found her buried beneath the ash. He placed a hand on her shoulder. "Blue," he said, giving her a firm but gentle shake.

Blue's gray eyes blinked open in a daze. She grabbed Valentine's arm, thinking he was an attacker.

"Blue! It's all right. It's me," said Valentine, trying to comfort her.

Blue rubbed her eyes and blinked several times, trying to regain focus. "Hey, Spooks," she said, cracking a pained smile.

"Let's get you out of here," said Valentine, picking her up in his arms. Turning to leave, they looked on in horror as a large plume of flames erupted from the south side of the city.

"The last bomb," Blue said softly. "I didn't make it in time."

Elliot walked toward Meier with both of his swords drawn. Meier threw another vial at him, but with a wave of his hand, he deflected it away. "It's over, Meier," he declared.

"Not from my perspective. Things have only just *begun*," Meier replied. He slowly stepped backward, looking around for an escape off the rooftop.

"What did you mean when you said we're all pawns in a bigger game?" asked Elliot.

"You really haven't figured it out?" Meier teased, still stepping backward.

"Figured *what* out?" Elliot was growing agitated. He closed the distance on Meier.

"You *really* think I had all the funds for this?" Meier asked. "I am simply a humble worker, carrying out the biddings of someone *much* bigger."

"*Who?*" Elliot demanded to know, raising his voice.

Meier looked over his shoulder and then turned back to Elliot and grimaced. "It really is a shame we couldn't work together on this," he said before leaping over the edge of the roof. He clung to a ladder on the side of the building and was making his way down at a quick pace.

Elliot rushed to the edge of the rooftop in time to see a group of police officers gather around the base of the ladder. He saw Meier reach for his belt for a vial, but before he could grab it, an officer raised his shotgun at Meier.

"Don't fire!" Elliot yelled. But it was too late. The sound of the blast echoed through the air.

Meier yelped in agony and fell to the ground, crushing not only the vials he was carrying but the override detonator for the bombs.

Looking up and to the south, Elliot saw a massive fireball stretch to the sky. "No ..." he said under his breath.

On the ground, Meier screamed and writhed in agony as the chemicals seeped into his skin. If you listened closely, you could almost hear the sound of his flesh sizzling and bubbling. Eventually though, much to Elliot's horror, Meier's agonizing screams turned to a disturbing and sadistic laughter. He rolled back and forth, roaring in a twisted laugh that made Elliot feel sick.

Elliot turned to an officer nearby. "Who shot him?" he asked in an accusatory tone.

"I-I did ..." said another officer. "I-it was a nonlethal round though. Our goal was just to knock him off the ladder."

"Well, you've certainly succeeded in *that*, as well as blowing up the south side of the city. He was carrying a detonator on him," Elliot scolded.

The commissioner interrupted before Elliot could continue ripping into the officer. "Where's the mayor?" he asked.

"Dead, Meier killed him," Elliot said bluntly.

The commissioner was about to speak but swallowed his words when he saw Valentine. "I suppose I really should be thanking you," he said. He extended a hand toward Valentine.

"I don't shake hands," replied the Reaper. "I suggest you get your men to the south and see if they can prevent *more* damage," Valentine said in a harsh tone.

The commissioner cleared his throat. "Right," he replied, retracting his hand.

"And, Commissioner, keep us out of your press release. I've wiped the hostages' memories. As far as they're concerned, the police did all the work." Valentine added. He turned his attention to Elliot, who was focused on Meier being loaded into an ambulance, strapped to the stretcher. "You all right, kid?" he asked.

"Hmm? Yeah, yeah, I'm fine." Elliot sighed. "I would've had him if it weren't for the cops. Why are you letting *them* take the credit, anyway?"

"I believe in maintaining a sense of anonymity," said Valentine, placing a hand on Elliot's cloaked shoulder. "None of this is your fault."

"I feel like it is," replied Elliot. "I could've prevented this," he said in a defeated tone.

"Meier will be going away for the rest of his life, I can assure you of that," said Valentine. "He'll pay for his crimes."

"It's not enough," replied Elliot. "How's Blue?" he asked, regaining a sense of the situation as a whole.

"A little bump on the head, but she's all right," said Valentine. "You did good today, kid."

"Novak?" Elliot asked.

Valentine reached into the pouch that hung from his belt and pulled out Novak's skull, showing it to Elliot.

"That's ... well, at least *he* got what he deserved."

Valentine put the skull back into the pouch. "Let's get the hell out of here," he said. "I could use a drink after this."

"What about the explosion on the south side?"

"We can't fight that virus," Valentine replied. "It's best we leave it to the emergency responders at this point."

CHAPTER 15

LOOSE ENDS

One week later

"It's been one week since the tragic attack that claimed over four hundred lives, though the official number is still unknown as the death toll continues to rise," said a news reporter.

Valentine sat on the couch in the den of his farmhouse watching TV, a cup of coffee in his right hand and his left arm propped up on the edge of the couch.

The reporter continued, "The perpetrator of the attack, a local chemist known as Doctor Adrian Meier, was apprehended by Sterling Police at the scene of the standoff at city hall. After taking him into custody, investigators have deemed Meier mentally unfit for trial, and he has been sent to the Hellings Psychiatric Hospital, where he will reside until a judge makes a verdict. Sterling City Police Commissioner James Lowell has since held this press conference."

The face of the female news anchor was replaced by footage of Commissioner Lowell. He stood in front of a podium among a large crowd. The collar of his jacket was pulled up around his neck to protect him from the cold wind. "It is with saddened and heavy hearts that we mourn the loss of lives of many great people, including our great mayor, Mister Wolf. I would like to invite you all to keep the memories of the lost and their families in your thoughts and prayers. As citizens of Sterling City, we are all one family, and we will mourn and prevail together as one. I would also like to take the time to thank the great men and women of the Sterling City Police. Their unwavering commitment to their duty to the city makes me proud as their commissioner, and I am proud to serve alongside each and every one of them. Your duty and service is deeply appreciated. Thank you." His speech was followed by an eruption of applause from the crowd of people before him. The camera panned over to a group of police officers, all in dress uniforms and standing at attention. They gave a simultaneous salute to their commissioner.

"Can you turn that shit off?" asked Elliot, entering the den.

Valentine took a sip of coffee, peering over the mug at Elliot. He was about to say something but bit his words back. He took another sip of coffee before turning off the television.

"Just don't wanna hear about it anymore," said Elliot.

"Considering going to see him?" Valentine asked.

Elliot nodded. "I think so. What do you think?" he asked.

Valentine shrugged. "Personally, I have no care in the matter."

"But what would *you* do?" Elliot pushed.

"I really don't know," Valentine replied, giving the thought a wave of dismissal. "I don't mean to be impartial; my mind is just elsewhere at the moment."

"I'll ask Warren," Elliot said, before turning and leaving.

"Keep him on track; he tends to wander off to war stories," Valentine called after him.

Sterling Cemetery was a place of beauty that attracted large numbers of photographers. It offered large trees with pink blossoms in the spring, immaculate tombs, and ornate statues of angels and animals. At night, the pathways were lit by old gas lamps.

The sun was barely above the tree line when Elliot arrived at the cemetery. A thick fog clung to the wet grass and marble headstones. Elliot walked quietly along the path, his hands buried in his jacket pockets and a hood pulled over his face. Eventually, he came to his destination. He took a seat in the wet grass and faced the headstone with his brother's name carved into it. He let out a heavy sigh, a pained look of sadness and remorse twisted his face. For a moment, he just listened to the birds singing in the distance. "I wish you were still here," he said to the headstone. Memories of Matthew flashed through his mind. He wished that he could go back to being a little kid, just for a little more time with his brother. A tear rolled down his left cheek. "I'm so sorry, Matthew. It should be me in this grave, not you." He put his face in his hands and ran his fingers through his hair. "Novak is dead, and Meier is in prison," he said, regaining his composure. "I promise, I'll find whoever's behind this. I hope you know I always looked up to you. You were the only true family I ever had. Thanks for always being there for me." He pulled a bottle of Matthew's favorite vodka from his coat. He removed the cap and poured some of the alcohol onto the grave before taking a large swig for himself. "Take care, big brother. I'll miss you." He sealed the bottle and leaned it against Matthew's headstone.

That night, Valentine sat in the shadows of a hospital room. He was dressed in his black cloak but had declined to take on the full form of the Reaper. He looked onward at the room's single occupant.

Bathed in the gray glow of the lights, an old woman lay fast asleep. Thin silver hair ran down to her shoulders. Medical tubes were attached to her paper skin by tape. Her sleeping breaths were in rhythm with the heart monitor, which beeped slowly. She stirred suddenly as if she had become aware that someone else was in the room with her. She turned over and faced the darker side of the room. Valentine emerged from the shadows, but instead of black, she perceived him in elegant robes of white. "I wondered if I would see you," she said in a weak voice.

"Hello, Gwen," said Valentine, forcing a pained smile. His heart beat faster, still yearning for his first love.

"Please," she said, trying to sit up. "Come sit." She moved a frail arm toward a nearby chair.

Valentine moved to her side. "Just rest," he said. He pulled the chair closer to the bedside and took a seat.

"You haven't aged a day," said Gwen, lifting a hand to touch Valentine's face.

"You're still as beautiful as the day I lost you," said Valentine. He took Gwen's hand in his and pressed it against his face. "Even after all these years, I still love you." There was a slight crack in his voice as a single tear rolled from his right eye.

"I thought about you often," said Gwen.

"As have I," replied Valentine. He reached into his robe and pulled out a worn black-and-white photograph. "I've kept this with me," he said, handing it to Gwen.

She took the photo and looked at it. "This is from ninety years ago," she said. "My, I've aged a lot."

"Not to me you haven't," said Valentine. He extended his right hand and caressed her face with the back of his fingers. "Listen … I-I'm sorry for not being the best that I could've. Losing you is a pain that I've carried with me for a long time."

"I wish things could have been different, Val. But you mustn't hold on to regret." Gwen rubbed her thumb on Valentine's cheek.

"I got over the regrets. I just … never got over the love." Valentine averted his eyes, avoiding contact.

"Part of me has always loved you, Val."

Valentine forced another smile. "How are you feeling?" he asked her.

"Weak." Gwen sighed. She looked down at her frail body before looking back up at Valentine. "Will it hurt?" she asked him.

"It'll be like you're falling asleep," replied Valentine.

"I'm glad I got to see you one last time." Gwen continued to caress his face.

"As am I." Another tear rolled down Valentine's cheek.

"Don't cry," said Gwen. "I'll find you in the next life." She pulled Valentine close with the little strength she had left.

Valentine placed his lips onto hers, caressing her face.

The gentle beeping of the heart monitor gave way to a constant ring.

"Goodbye, Gwen," said Valentine.

Adorned in his black cloak and tunic, his hood pulled over his white skull, Elliot made his way through the halls of Hellings Hospital.

The floors and walls were made from stone that never retained heat. The patients—or "residents," as the employees preferred to say—were all kept in primitive observation rooms.

Prisoners, Elliot thought to himself.

The empty screams and wails of the patients echoed endlessly through the halls.

Some of the patients lunged at Elliot as he passed by their cells, forcibly throwing themselves against their cages, trying desperately to grab on to his cloak. Just like in the lab, they begged for mercy; they begged for death.

One patient was wrapped in a straitjacket; he sat in the front of his cell, banging his head against the bars even after his skull had started to bleed.

Elliot materialized through a steel door at the end of the hall and then another. He made his way over to the far side of the facility where the most dangerous "patients" were kept. Elliot entered a hallway that had a series of secured doors. At the end of the hallway was a single cell. He slid the view hatch open and peered inside. He couldn't see anyone, but he could hear what sounded like someone muttering to himself. He permeated through the door and entered the cell.

Meier sat on the floor, restrained by a jacket and facing the corner. He rocked back and forth in the shadow of the room, muttering to himself incoherently.

As Elliot crept closer, he could start to make out Meier's words. It was like he was having a full conversation with himself.

"He's here … He's here! But what does he want? Has he come for me? He's coming … He's coming." Meier burst out in a maniacal cackle that shook Elliot. "He's here, he's here, he's here. Closer … closer …" Meier laughed again. "He's coming for me!" he cackled again. He spun around quickly and faced Elliot. The right side of his face had been burned by Blue, and his right eye was white. His mouth was twisted into a horrid grin that stretched from ear to ear. In his left eye was the beaming glow of insanity.

Elliot realized that the root of his condition was the chemical vials that had broken when he fell. They had completely destroyed his brain, twisted and remolded it. Elliot knelt down and looked at him.

Meier looked like he was about to say something but instead burst out in laughter.

Elliot was angry. He wanted to kill Meier. Had he gotten the chance to kill him at the city hall, he would have. But now, he almost pitied him. Not only was he locked in a prison cell, but he was locked in a cell of his own machination, stuck in the confines of his own mind—a man who had set out to destroy a city but in the end had destroyed himself. "More suitable than death," Elliot said to Meier.

Valentine greeted Elliot outside of Hellings. "How'd it go?" he asked.

Elliot didn't reply; he was somewhat lost in thought at the moment.

"Get any answers from him?" Valentine asked.

"Huh?" Elliot refocused. "No, no. He, uh, wasn't really in any condition to speak."

Valentine paused in thought for a moment before he asked his next question, unsure of what he wanted to hear. "Did you kill him?" he finally asked.

After a moment of silence, Elliot answered, "I wanted to." He turned and looked back at the hospital. "Just couldn't find it in myself. In a sense, he's already done it to himself."

Valentine put a hand on his shoulder. "You did good, kid. You've come a long way."

"I'm not sure how I feel. But like you said, sometimes it's best to let go," said Elliot. "How did your thing go?" he asked, changing the subject.

"It went. Like you, not really sure how I feel about it," Valentine replied.

Before Valentine could continue, a call came through his stolen police radio. "All units, we have a bank robbery in progress. Multiple armed suspects. Caution is advised."

Valentine looked at Elliot.

"Lead the way," said Elliot.

The alarms in the bank were blaring, and the police had not yet arrived when Elliot and Valentine got there. They entered through the front doors into the main lobby. A siren wailed as red strobes flashed around the interior of the building.

Valentine spotted a smashed door that led to a hallway in the back. "Let's try and take them by surprise," he said to Elliot.

Elliot responded with a single nod and followed close behind Valentine.

They could hear voices coming from the end of the hall. The vault door was open, and three men were putting stacks of money into duffel bags as fast as they could. Two more men stood outside the vault as guards.

One of the guards could see a silhouette at the end of the hall, and the lights began to flicker violently. Scared, he fired his weapon down the hallway, spooking the other men. They quickly grabbed the bags of money and started to make a run for it.

Elliot, who was at the end of the hall, sped toward the guards in a blinding blur. Landing behind them, he grabbed each of them by the head and slammed them to the ground. He levitated the bodies and tossed them into the vault.

Valentine emerged from the shadows and knocked the three other men back into the vault with a black force. Using his powers, he closed the vault door and sealed it.

"Good shit," remarked Elliot.

"All right, let's go meet the boys in blue," said Valentine.

Police officers were entering the lobby with their weapons drawn. Commissioner James Lowell was moving behind his men. He holstered his weapon when he saw Elliot and Valentine.

"Figures you two are here," said the commissioner. "Leave another bloody mess everywhere?"

"Actually, surprisingly no," said Valentine, almost as if mocking the commissioner. "They're all in the vault. Probably pretty anxious for your men to get them out." He tilted his head in a subtle implication.

Lowell raised his head in realization and appreciation. "Thank you …"

"Reaper," said Valentine.

"And you?" asked Lowell, turning to Elliot.

"Shadow," answered Valentine before Elliot could.

"Y'know, we really couldn't have taken Meier without you. I've … come to appreciate our partnership," said Lowell.

"As have I," replied Valentine. "As usual, keep us out of the press."

Lowell cracked a smile. "Of course. See you 'round."

"You can count on it," said Valentine.

Elliot sat out on the patio of the farmhouse. His dog, who now stood at waist height, was resting his head on Elliot's lap. He ran his fingers through his thick black fur.

Valentine came out onto the patio, a cup of coffee in hand. "Pick a name yet?" he asked Elliot. He knelt down and scratched the dog's head.

"Sable," Elliot replied.

"It's a good name. I like it. Fitting," said Valentine.

"Yeah." Elliot let out a deep sigh. "S'pose Bex and I should get out of your hair now, eh?"

"Y'know, I've been thinking about that," said Valentine, taking a seat in a patio chair. He rested his coffee on a small table to his left. "I want to recover as many relics as I can and destroy them so they can never be found. Could use someone to look over the house."

"What about Warren? He can look after the house," asked Elliot.

"Well, who's gonna look after him? Crazy bastard might impale himself on something."

Elliot chuckled. "True," he said. "But shouldn't we both go?" he asked.

"Someone needs to protect Sterling City while I'm gone. I think that should be you."

"You really think I can?" Elliot's voice had a touch of doubt in it.

"I think you're more than capable," Valentine assured him. He stood up and extended a hand to Elliot.

Elliot stood up and shook his hand.

"Don't burn the house down while I'm gone." Valentine turned to walk away but stopped. "Oh, just remembered. Wanted to give you this." Valentine reached into his jacket pocket and pulled out the small bag he usually wore on his belt.

"What is this?" Elliot asked, taking the pouch.

"Won it in a bet. It's a bottomless bag. Comes in handy."

"Thanks." Elliot smirked. "Careful out there."

"Take care, kid," said Valentine, firmly shaking Elliot's hand.

EPILOGUE

AFTERMATH

One month later

Elliot walked through the city with his dog, Sable, at his side. A fresh, delicate snow was falling and dusting the concrete sidewalk. The snow crunched softly with each step that he took.

Sable kept up with him at a moderate pace, leaving large, bear-like prints in the fresh snow.

He stopped outside of a café. The lit interior cast a light on the snow, turning it into a shimmering gold blanket on the sidewalk. Elliot looked into one of the large windows and saw May sitting at a table, eating with her boyfriend. He watched them, and for a moment, he was lost in the memories of when he used to take her there. It had been their favorite little spot. He left and made his way down the street before he brought attention to himself. He pulled up his collar and tightened it around his neck to block the snow. His walk had taken him to the part of the city where Meier's bomb had detonated.

"One thousand people lost their lives and another two thousand have been displaced from their homes," the news reporter had said.

Over six square city blocks on the south side had been condemned by the local government. What once was the thriving center of the south was now an empty ghost town of scorched buildings and memories. Buildings at the epicenter of the explosion had been reduced to rubble. Reports said the most casualties took place there. The buildings surrounding the epicenter were still standing on their foundations but had been charred by the fire that ravaged them.

Long pieces of bright-yellow caution tape marked off areas that were deemed hazardous because of the large amounts of the chemical that had collected in spots. Some parts of the streets and building were permanently stained a faded green from the toxic cloud that had rolled through the streets after the explosion.

Evidence of a mass exodus littered the streets. Abandoned cars, suitcases, clothes, and other belongings had been forgotten and left behind by their owners in their panic-stricken rush from the area.

Elliot picked up a small doll that had been left behind. For a moment, he stared at it, forgetting where he was. "Did they survive?" he wondered. The feeling of guilt still weighed heavy on his shoulders. For weeks, he had replayed the scene over and over and over in his head, trying desperately to imagine a better outcome. "What could I have done differently?" he often asked himself. Part of him felt like he had failed the city and, worse yet, his brother. Sometimes he could almost feel Matthew's hand on his shoulder, or he might hear him whisper in the breeze that rolled by.

Sable hunched low to the ground and let out a soft growl. Sharp, pointed ears faced forward, attuned on a silhouetted figure that walked among the debris.

Elliot, coming to his senses, faced the same direction as Sable and looked at the figure ahead of him. He let out the darkness that dwelled within him, donning the appearance of the Reaper as a thick black smoke washed over him.

A thick black smoke washed over Sable, clinging to his fur and transforming him into a beast from the depths of the darkness, a large, fanged black dog with a bare skull. His size was comparable to that of a black bear.

Elliot stuck out his right hand, keeping Sable at bay. He loosened his left hand's grip on the doll he was holding, letting it fall and rest in the snow. He glided silently over the snow, making his way toward the dark figure in the distance, not leaving any tracks in the snow behind him.

"Ah, it's you," said the figure. It was Commissioner Lowell. "Out for a stroll?" he asked Elliot.

"Same as you?" Elliot responded.

"I haven't been able to sleep. This whole thing, it … it haunts me. It'll always be a scar on this city." Lowell kicked his foot at the charred rubble on the ground. "Would've been a lot worse had it not been for you. Speaking of which …" He looked around before finishing his sentence. "Where's your partner?"

"Taking care of some personal things," Elliot replied.

Lowell looked at the beast who sat loyally by Elliot's side but didn't comment. He let out a heavy sigh and drew a cigarette from his coat pocket. He lit it and took a long drag. He watched the smoke drift into the sky before he spoke again. "Have a good night," he said with a nod.

Elliot nodded back but didn't speak. He looked at the falling snow and what had collected on the ground. It had been three years since he had seen snow, and he had never missed it. It was however only two weeks until Christmas, and he had very much missed that.

Henry Folds, who was now Sterling City's newest mayor, had invited him and Rebecca to his estate for the holidays.

Though Elliot was looking forward to it, Christmas just wouldn't be the same without Matthew.

A call came through the police radio on Elliot's belt. "All units, we have reports of a large disturbance on the east side at the Sterling Bank. Alarms have been triggered, and there are several injured. Suspect is unknown but assumed to be armed and dangerous. Caution is advised."

Elliot looked down at Sable. "Let's go, buddy."

Several police officers had gathered outside Sterling Bank and had secured a perimeter around the building. A large crowd of pedestrians had gathered to watch the injured victims be loaded into ambulances.

When Elliot arrived on the scene, he saw steaming pools of an odd-colored liquid. Upon further observation he saw that the liquid was slowly eating away at the pavement. He looked up and saw several smashed windows and metal doors that looked as though they had melted off their hinges. Drawing his swords, he stepped on pieces of shattered glass that crunched beneath his boots and entered the bank.

Elliot could see evidence of the same corrosive liquid inside the bank.

Large holes had been eaten into the floor, their edges still bubbling and smoking. The bank vault had a large melted hole in the center. He could hear a shuffling movement from within the vault.

A glowing yellow humanoid creature climbed out from within the vault. Each step it took left a pool of the liquid that burned through the floor. It lifted its head up toward Elliot to reveal glowing green eyes and a wide, toothless mouth. Parts of rotten flesh and skull could be seen on its head. It let out a gargled moan before speaking in a growl. "Hello, Shadow."

"What the fuck kind of abomination are *you* supposed to be?" asked Elliot.

"Mmm, I resent that," the creature growled. "Allow me to introduce myself," it said, standing up tall, its height and shoulder width nearly double that of Elliot. "I am Caustic!" the creature yelled, expelling a powerful stream of acid at Elliot.

Elliot walked through the cemetery, his hands in his pockets and his head hung low. When he looked up, he saw an old man standing at Matthew's grave. "Um, hello?" he asked the man.

The old man turned. "You must be Elliot," he said.

"How do you know me?" Elliot asked. "Who are you?"

"I'm your father."

Printed in the United States
by Baker & Taylor Publisher Services